THE CRADLE CONSPIRACY

CHRISTY BARRITT

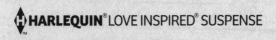

Recycling programs
for this product may
not exist in your area.

LOVE INSPIRED BOOKS

ISBN-13: 978-1-335-67912-3

The Cradle Conspiracy

www.Harlequin.com

Printed in U.S.A.

"Make another move and she dies," the gunman growled.

Sienna cried out, her eyes wide and brimming with fear.

"You don't have to do this." Devin paused, knowing he needed to tread carefully.

"Where's the boy?" the man demanded. "I'll only let her go if I get the boy back. Your choice." The man jerked Sienna closer, gun to her still.

"You're not getting your hands on that child," Devin said. "And you're not going to go anywhere with Sienna, either."

Sirens sounded in the distance, and the gunman straightened. "This isn't over," the man muttered.

With one last glare, the intruder shoved Sienna into Devin's arms and darted out the window.

Devin grasped Sienna's shoulders. "Are you okay?"

She nodded. "Colby..."

"He's safe. At the neighbors'. Now I need to go after this guy."

Devin slipped around her and darted out the window after the gunman. Before he could reach the man's fleeing figure, a car pulled up. The man jumped inside.

And he was gone.

Christy Barritt's books have won a Daphne du Maurier Award for Excellence in Suspense and Mystery and have been twice nominated for an RT Reviewers' Choice Best Book Award. She's married to her Prince Charming, a man who thinks she's hilarious—but only when she's not trying to be. Christy's a self-proclaimed klutz, an avid music lover and a road-trip aficionado. For more information, visit her website at christybarritt.com.

I will lift up mine eyes unto the hills, from whence cometh my help. My help cometh from the Lord, which made heaven and earth.
—*Psalm* 121:1-2

This book is dedicated to those who are
facing mountains they feel like they'll never conquer.

ONE

Sienna Thompson lay in bed, trying to get to sleep.

But she couldn't rest. She hadn't been able to get any shut-eye for the past two days.

How could she sleep knowing that something terrible might have happened to her friend Anita? Little two-year-old Colby's life would never be the same if something happened to his mama.

So why couldn't Sienna get in touch with the woman?

Anita was supposed to pick up Colby on Monday. Today was Wednesday, and Sienna had heard nothing from the boy's mom. An ominous feeling churned in her gut, and she tried to push away the worst-case scenarios that flooded her mind.

A car accident? Medical emergency? Had she been the victim of some kind of crime?

Maybe the answer was simpler. Maybe Anita was just irresponsible. Maybe she'd lost track of time. Or maybe it was just as simple as Sienna misunderstanding her.

As Sienna turned over in bed, a sound at the other side of the house caught her ear.

What was that noise? She hoped Colby hadn't somehow gotten out of his crib.

Sienna threw her legs out of bed and tugged a sweatshirt on over her T-shirt and yoga pants. With quick—but quiet—steps, she hurried into the hallway and paused, waiting to listen.

There was the noise again. It almost sounded like a scratch—and a grating one, at that.

Concern began to rise in her.

She rushed across the hallway toward her guest room, where Colby had been sleeping soundly only thirty minutes ago when Sienna had put him down.

She cracked his door open and saw the boy still in the crib, his chest rising and falling peacefully. Pausing for a second, Sienna could hear the sweet, reassuring sound of him breathing.

Sienna released the air from her lungs. The boy was asleep still. And he was okay.

So what had that noise been? Just a scratch in the night? Maybe a critter beneath her house? That had happened a couple years ago, and an exterminator had discovered a stray cat in her crawl space.

Sienna wasn't normally given to paranoia, but the hair on her arms seemed to rise with each second that ticked past. Her gut told her that was no cat. No, the noise sounded too close. Too loud. Too consistent.

Swallowing her anxiety, Sienna grabbed the only potential weapon she could find—a rolling pin. It was also known as Colby's new favorite toy. She'd left it on the hallway table, telling herself she'd put it away in the morning when she wasn't so exhausted. Being the only caregiver of an active two-year-old was more exhausting than she would have guessed.

Carefully, Sienna crept down the hallway. Her senses were on hyperdrive as she listened again for some signal to confirm her gut instinct that something was wrong.

All she heard was silence.

She tiptoed into her living room and froze.

The window above an armchair was open, and a cool summer breeze slithered inside. Sienna wouldn't have left it open. She never slept with the windows cracked—not as a single lady.

She stepped into the shadow of her hallway where the effervescent moonlight couldn't reach her and scanned her surroundings.

Something or someone had opened that window.

She needed to figure out what or who, and she needed to figure it out quickly.

Something moved near the wall across the room.

A figure.

In her house.

Creeping toward her.

Sienna swallowed a scream. She didn't want to awaken Colby and upset him—even if every instinct in her wanted to panic. No, she had to keep a cool head for Colby's sake.

Her limbs trembled as she slunk back down the hallway toward Colby's room.

Just as she reached his door, she looked back. The dark figure appeared at the end of the hallway. He wore a black ski mask. But Sienna could still see the reflection of his eyes as his gaze hit her.

Something about the gleam confirmed that this man was no good. He was dangerous. And he was coming for her.

Please, God. Help us!

She sucked in a breath and darted into Colby's room. Her hands shook as she grabbed the lock. She had to twist the mechanism in place before the man got here. Before he got *them*. Yet nothing cooperated.

No, no, no!

Finally, Sienna's fingers got the grip they needed, and the lock turned in place.

Thank You, Lord.

But Sienna knew the flimsy metal barrier wouldn't last long. She'd picked locks like these as a child, using only a bobby pin, while pretending she was a spy. The memory didn't comfort her now.

Turning, she glanced around, searching for something—anything—that would protect them. There was nothing but a lamp, a dresser, a twin-size bed and a portable crib.

Her heart raced. Why hadn't she grabbed her phone?

Sienna hadn't thought she would need it. Worst-case scenario, she'd thought she'd have to rock Colby back to sleep. Never had she imagined this.

The dresser, she realized. She needed to move it in front of the door. It was wooden, solid and heavy and could serve as a blockade.

Without thinking about it more, Sienna shoved her hip against it. Slowly, the furniture scooted across the wooden floor.

As she inched it forward, the doorknob rattled. Not just rattled. Rattled furiously. Unrelentingly.

She sucked in a quick breath of air.

The man on the other side wanted in. Why couldn't he just take whatever he wanted and leave? Not that Sienna had much in terms of material possessions. In fact, she hardly had anything. No money. No jewelry. Nothing of true value.

That was when the truth hit Sienna.

He must want her. Or Colby.

Her lungs tightened.

No, no, no… Neither of those options was acceptable. Especially not Colby.

The sound of the man ramming against the door filled the earlier quiet.

Scarier still, the man himself remained silent—chillingly silent. He hadn't said a word, yet his actions said plenty. It was the kind of quiet that made Sienna's mind fill in the gaps with terrible yet unverified truths.

Sienna found a burst of strength and shoved the dresser the rest of the way in front of the door—and just in time.

The door frame began to split.

She swung her head toward the crib. The noises were waking Colby.

It was just as well. The two of them needed to get out of here.

Now.

The window, Sienna realized. It was the only way out. Her only solution and means of escape. But she had to move quickly.

At least her house was only one story. If she climbed outside with Colby, the landing shouldn't be too bad. She could protect the baby when they hit the grass below.

The door frame cracked again, sending another pulse of fear through her.

She scooped Colby up in her arms and rushed toward the window, where a dark summer sky stared back.

She kissed the top of Colby's soft head, praying he wouldn't feel her terror and feed off it.

The door frame cracked again, and the dresser moved a couple of inches. The intruder was almost inside.

Sienna bit back a scream, unlatched the window and thrust it up just as the man shoved the dresser out of the way. He burst into the room, his gun pointed right at Sienna.

Her life and all her unfulfilled dreams flashed before her eyes. But even more, she pictured Colby's future. He deserved a future, and no one was going to take that away.

Devin Matthews blinked, wondering if he'd started to fall asleep on his back deck. The full moon shone around him, illuminating the suburban neighborhood more than usual. But the shadows within the moonlight made him tense.

There was no wind out here tonight. Not even a breeze. So what was that movement in his neighbor's backyard?

It could be a raccoon or a fox, he supposed. Or maybe his neighbor had taken some trash out. He'd never seen the woman as a night owl, and it was already almost midnight.

His restlessness was a complication of not being able to sleep. It didn't matter how cold or hot it was outside, Devin often found himself on his back deck, staring at the stars, and thinking about life until the wee hours of the morning.

These times were his solitude—and possibly his undoing. Devin had to get back into a schedule. He had to return to the land of the living. But doing so was much harder than he'd ever anticipated. Grief always remained at a close enough distance that his life felt stuck at a standstill.

He'd taken a two-month leave of absence from the FBI in order to get himself straight. The way it was looking, it might take more than two months. In fact, maybe he should look for another job, one that didn't remind him so much of the tragedies of his past.

He glanced at his neighbor's place again. Devin wasn't trying to be nosy. But his deck happened to be high enough that he could see the woman's patio and back door.

And he'd thought he saw a shadow moving there again.

He waited. Listened. Stood for a better look.

All was silent—at least it was from where he had positioned himself.

Devin knew his neighbor was single, but he tried to not talk to anyone unless necessary. He'd moved here a year ago, and Sienna Thompson had moved in six months later. The two had briefly met when she'd come over to introduce herself, but all it had taken was one encounter, and she hadn't bothered to try and get to know him again.

And that was fine because Devin wasn't interested in having a social life—not in the least. He was ready for a clean slate. A new start. By himself.

But he hadn't been able to avoid noticing that Sienna seemed like the iconic girl next door.

The woman was happy. Cheerful. Friendly. Not to mention nice to look at it in a sweet, modest way.

Except for the past week—the woman had had a baby with her. Out of the blue.

Why was that? Was the baby a nephew? Had she adopted?

Devin, you're just seeing things where there isn't anything. You're used to crime being around every corner when it's not. This neighborhood is safe.

He ran a hand over his face, trying to clear his thoughts.

No sooner had he done so than a scream cut through the air.

Devin's mind wasn't playing tricks on him after all. Someone was in trouble.

He sprinted across the lawn. When he got a better look at Sienna's house, he sucked in a breath. A window was open and someone hung out.

Sienna.

She screamed again, and his heart surged. He had to help. Now.

"Take him!" she yelled.

The next thing he knew, Sienna thrust the baby out the window. The boy screamed and kicked—obviously frightened. A shadow moved behind her.

Devin darted toward her and took the boy from her outstretched arms. He started to reach for Sienna, too, when someone jerked her back inside. More shouting sounded. A scream. A crack.

His pulse thrummed harder.

Devin couldn't simply set this child down and expect him to be safe. His gut twisted as he briefly considered his options. The child or Sienna. He didn't have time to ponder them too long.

Both, he decided.

He darted across the street, suddenly wishing he *had* been more social. He pounded on the Wilsons' door. Finally the sixtysomething woman answered, her gaze hazy with sleep. Her eyes widened quickly when she saw Devin.

"Can I help you?" The retired woman pulled her housecoat tighter.

He placed the baby in her arms—no time for formalities. "Watch him. Lock your doors. Call the police. Understand?"

She opened her mouth as if to ask questions, but instead muttered in a shaky voice, "Okay."

Devin didn't have time to expound or be polite. Not now.

No, he had to move before Sienna ended up with a bullet through her heart.

He rushed across the street just in time to hear another scream and a man's voice raging, "Why did you have to do that?"

He reached the front door and tried the knob. It was locked. Of course.

Using all his strength, Devin jammed his shoulder into the wood. Nothing happened on the first try. He did it again and again and again until finally the wood cracked. Cracked some more. Cracked enough that he was able to dart into the house and toward the room where he heard Sienna screaming.

He stopped in his tracks when he saw a gunman standing there. His weapon pressed against Sienna's head.

"Make another move, and she dies," the man growled.

Sienna cried out, her eyes wide and brimming with a fear so big Devin could see it even in the darkness.

"You don't have to do this." Devin paused, knowing he needed to tread carefully. Wishing he'd had time to grab his gun.

"Where's the boy?" the man demanded.

"He's somewhere safe." Devin wasn't about to give up the child's location.

"I'll only let her go if I get the boy back. Your choice." The man jerked Sienna closer, gun to her head still. She let out another cry, her terror palpable in the small space.

"You're not getting your hands on that child," Devin said. "And you're not going to go anywhere with Sienna, either."

The gunman chuckled. "You're not the one calling the shots right now."

Sirens sounded in the distance, and the gunman straightened.

He'd heard them, too. Was rethinking his strategy. Hopefully realizing there was no way out.

Devin prayed this situation wouldn't escalate.

"This isn't over," the man muttered.

With one last glare, the intruder shoved Sienna into Devin's arms and darted out the window.

Devin grasped Sienna's shoulders, pulling her back until he saw her face. "Are you okay?"

She nodded, though barely. "Colby…"

"He's safe. At the neighbors'. Now I need to go after this guy."

Sienna didn't argue.

Devin slipped around her and darted out the window after the gunman. Before he could reach the man's fleeing figure, a car pulled up. The man jumped inside.

And he was gone.

But not before Devin memorized the license plate.

TWO

All Sienna could think about was Colby. She needed to see him for herself. To know that he was okay.

It didn't matter that her limbs were a quivering mess. That tears streamed down her cheeks. That she was shaken to her core.

All that mattered was this child who wasn't even hers. Colby was her responsibility until Anita returned, and the boy had quickly gained a place in her heart.

She darted past the displaced dresser. Around the cracked door frame. Through her once comforting, safe home. Chilly summer air hit her as she stepped onto the porch.

She was halfway across her lawn when someone jerked her to a stop. She lurched her head around and saw Devin standing there.

Devin.

Her handsome neighbor who never spoke. Or

smiled. Or even waved. He had, however, just saved her life.

"Are you okay?" He studied her with his gaze, something close to worry lingering in his eyes. His chest rose and fell rapidly with exertion. What had happened?

"I'm fine," she gasped, realizing she was breathless herself. "Where's the intruder? Did you catch him?"

"He had a car waiting for him. He got away."

Her spirits sank so quickly that her stomach ached. That man was still out there. That meant she and Colby were still in danger. "I need to see Colby."

"Wait a minute." Devin didn't release her arm yet, and his intense gaze remained on her. "Take a few deep breaths."

"What? Why?" Had he lost his mind? Sienna needed to see the child she'd been entrusted to take care of.

Devin leveled his gaze with her, his voice surprisingly reassuring. "The baby is okay. But you need to calm down before you take him or you'll frighten him."

Sienna started to argue but stopped herself. Devin was right. She *was* a mess right now, and her legs might turn to gelatin at any minute. She needed to get herself together.

With Devin's hand still gripping her arm, she closed her eyes. Inhaled deeply. Exhaled.

Sienna repeated the process before she opened her eyes, feeling more collected.

"Thank you," she muttered, her gaze fluttering up to meet Devin's.

"I'll walk you over." Devin kept a hand on her arm as they crossed the street.

He deposited her at the front door of the Wilsons' house just as the cops pulled up. He squeezed her arm and murmured a few more reassurances before meeting the officers and explaining what had happened.

But Sienna hardly heard any of it. No, the door opened, and her gaze fell on Colby as he rested in Mrs. Wilson's arms.

Colby.

Sweet Colby.

Her heart melted into a puddle of relief.

Thankfully, the boy seemed calm and peaceful as he hugged a stuffed bunny rabbit. But as soon as he saw Sienna, he reached his chubby little arms out toward her. Just what she'd been waiting for.

She took the boy into her embrace and held him close—but not close enough to scare him. As soon as the clean scent of baby shampoo and lotion filled her, her heart rate slowed even more.

He was okay. They were okay. For now.

But what if that man came back? Sienna would think about that more later. Right now, she wanted to concentrate on Colby and getting warm.

"Hello, little one," she murmured.

Tears filled her eyes as the boy rested his head on her shoulder.

He was okay, she told herself again.

Thank goodness.

Things could have turned out a lot differently.

Thankfully, Devin had shown up when he did.

But Sienna knew this was far from over.

The break-in hadn't been random. No, someone had specifically wanted Colby, and Sienna had no idea why.

Did this have something to do with Anita's disappearance?

She knew the likely answer was yes.

Now she had to figure out what to do about it. Because Sienna would keep this boy safe if it was the last thing she did.

Devin glanced over from the officers he was speaking with into the Wilsons' house, which had become an unofficial meeting place. The kind couple had said it was okay, and it was better than everyone—mostly Sienna and Colby—being outside in the unusually chilly June evening.

A CSI team was inside Sienna's place, collecting evidence. Another team talked to neighbors, while yet another officer ran the plates on the car that had driven off.

Devin had already given his statement, but

officers were giving Sienna a few minutes to recover before telling her side of the story. The Wilsons had made themselves scarce, fixing coffee for everyone in the kitchen and staying out of the police's way.

His heart caught when he saw Sienna cradling Colby. The boy had fallen asleep in her arms, and she looked down at him with such a look of love in her gaze. The moment reminded him of Grace and Willow, and sadness gripped him so furiously that his chest ached.

It still seemed impossible that the two were gone.

He pushed those thoughts aside. This wasn't the time to explore his grief.

Instead, he glanced at Sienna and the baby again. What was the story between these two? He was more curious than ever.

He'd have to wait until later to find out.

Sienna looked paler as Detective Jenson approached. Devin watched her a moment. Noted her slender figure. Her wheat-colored hair with subtle blond highlights. How her wavy locks brushed her shoulders, and how the few scattered freckles across her nose gave her a youthful appearance.

The woman was easy on the eyes, for sure.

And she was terrified right now.

Devin made a split-second decision and went to sit on the couch beside her. Though Sienna held the baby, she looked so utterly alone. Something unknown to him seemed to drive him for answers.

"You mind if I listen in?" he asked softly.

Sienna's eyes widened with surprise before she shook her head. "No, not at all. I…owe you."

"You don't owe me anything. I'm just glad I got there when I did." He looked at the detective for approval. "You okay with me staying?"

"Yes, sir." Detective Jenson's gaze fell on Sienna as he pulled a ladder-back chair from the corner of the living room and placed it three feet in front of her. "Ma'am, could you talk me through what happened?"

Devin listened as Sienna told him about hearing a sound. Checking on Colby. Going into her living room and seeing the window open. Making it to Colby before the man saw her.

Thankfully, the woman was quick on her feet. Otherwise tonight could have ended a lot differently. This could have been a very different kind of crime scene. His stomach turned at the thought.

"You have no idea who the man was?" Detective Jenson kept his voice professional but kind as he leaned toward Sienna.

"No idea. Of course I couldn't see his face— he wore a mask—but I didn't recognize his voice, either. Or his eyes." Sienna's voice cracked as memories appeared to pummel her.

"Tell me about your son."

Sienna looked down at Colby and smiled—but it was a sad, wistful smile. "Oh, he's not mine. He's a coworker's."

Both men stared at her, waiting for her to explain.

She let out a small sigh, one that belied the simplicity of her words.

"A woman I work with—her name is Anita Gwinn—asked me if I could take care of Colby for a week. She had to go out of town to attend to her mother, who just had hip replacement surgery and needed round-the-clock care."

"Is this Anita Gwinn woman a coworker or a friend?" Devin asked, trying to get a better feel for the situation.

Coworker sounded cold and impersonal. People usually didn't trust acquaintances with their children. In Devin's experience, at least.

Sienna hesitated and glanced at Colby again. "Honestly, more of a coworker. I know that sounds terrible to say. But I don't know Anita all that well. She only moved to the area a few months ago, and she said she didn't have anyone else to ask."

"Where do you work?"

"I teach kindergarten. Anita was a teaching assistant in the classroom next door, but she seemed to latch on to me for some reason."

"What was she like?"

"She's probably in her early thirties. She's kind of frazzled, but she is a single mom, so I figured that was why. No mention of a boyfriend or the baby's father. But she loves Colby. Had pictures on her desk and on her phone. Everywhere. She always said he was the one good thing in her life."

"Did anything seem off about her?"

Sienna shrugged. "Anita was quirky. But some people are, right? I mean… I don't know. I just want to give her the benefit of the doubt."

"We should probably call Ms. Gwinn," Jenson said. "Would you mind giving me her number? I'd like to talk to her."

"Of course." Sienna hesitated and shifted. "But here's the thing—Anita was supposed to pick Colby up two days ago. She never showed up, and she hasn't been answering her phone."

Devin's heart rate kicked up a notch. Most likely, when combined with what had happened tonight, that wasn't a coincidence.

"Did you call the police?" Jenson asked.

"No, I figured Anita would show up. Or that she lost track of time. Or… I don't really know. I was at a loss as to what to do. I didn't want a social worker to come and take Colby, though. I figured he was better off with me until his mom returned. Maybe, looking back, that wasn't wise." Sienna frowned as she glanced at the detective and then Devin, her gaze begging for understanding yet laced with regret.

Jenson straightened, and Devin could tell he was skeptical about Sienna's story. It did seem like a strange explanation, yet it could still be plausible. Police often investigated those closest to the case first. Nine times out of ten, it was someone familiar instead of a stranger.

"We'll need you to be available in case we have any more questions," Jenson said.

"Of course." Sienna offered a tight nod, but her gaze showed her exhaustion.

As the detective walked away, Devin turned toward Sienna. He knew this wasn't any of his business. But he couldn't stop himself from saying what needed to be said. All of his FBI training begged for his attention.

"I realize this isn't my place, but I don't think you should stay at your house tonight," he said. "It's not safe."

"That could be true, but I'm not sure where else I can go."

The thought of them being in a hotel made Devin's stomach churn. Sienna and Colby were too much of a target, and hotels weren't secure. They needed more answers before Sienna resumed life as normal. Or even halfway normal.

"This is going to sound strange." Devin kept

his voice professional. "I know it will. But I have a family cabin about an hour from here. Why don't you use it?"

"I'm not sure the idea of staying in a cabin miles from nowhere is comforting." A moment of fear flickered in her gaze, and she glanced back down at Colby again.

Devin wanted to ask her if there was anyone else she could stay with. But he didn't. Because he knew that not anyone else would do. Sienna needed protection—at least until they had more answers.

Devin had seen the gunman with his own eyes. He'd seen the ruthlessness in his gaze. Heard the malice in his voice. Devin knew that whoever he was, the man would go to extreme lengths to get what he wanted. And what he wanted was Colby.

Devin was desperate to piece this together. Who was the man? Why did he want the baby? And where was this baby's mom?

When he put it all together, he didn't like the picture it formed.

The situation was full of danger and ruthlessness.

"Listen, I'm FBI," Devin started. "I'm currently on a leave of absence from the bureau, and I don't have anything on my schedule. If you're comfortable with it, I can stand guard while you're there at the cabin."

Sienna still hesitated. "I don't want to put you out."

"I can't exactly sit back and resume life while my neighbor and an innocent child are threatened."

When she still didn't agree, Devin softened his stance and his tone. If he'd only been a little friendlier, maybe she wouldn't be so untrusting right now.

"Do you have a better alternative?" Devin asked. "Because as long as I know the two of you are safe, I'm okay. I can stand down."

Sienna glanced at Colby again before shaking her head. "Not really. I have friends I could stay with…but most of them have kids, and I don't want to put anyone else in danger. I have to look out for Colby. I really don't know what to do."

"Just take me up on the offer. I promise, the invitation is purely professional."

Finally she nodded. "Okay. For Colby's sake, I'll do it. But please don't make me regret it."

Just then, Detective Jenson walked back into the room, a grim look on his face. His eyes went to Sienna, some of that earlier doubt still there— and still strong.

Devin braced himself for whatever he had to say.

"We're trying to locate Anita Gwinn," he

announced. "The bad news is that Anita Gwinn doesn't appear to have existed until four months ago."

THREE

Devin felt the tension pulling across his shoulders as he drove into the night with Sienna beside him and Colby sleeping in a car seat in the back of his SUV.

They'd left the warm lights of suburbia and headed west, deeper into the Rocky Mountains. Homes and businesses were sparser out here, making it ideal as a hiding spot. Yet these mountains within themselves were a beautiful danger, one that needed to be appreciated and respected.

Devin had grown up in Colorado, almost five hours away from this area, but had moved here when the FBI stationed him in Denver. His little town of Woodard's Mill was on the outskirts of the city and felt like the perfect place to relax after a stressful day at work—whenever he finally went back to work. Things like this didn't happen in neighborhoods like his.

Except this had happened. Right next door.

He couldn't stop reviewing tonight's events.

Why things had played out as they had. What this story could possibly be. Those questions were what motivated him to solve every case he'd been handed while working in the criminal investigative division: answers that would ultimately lead to justice.

He glanced over at Sienna, at her heavy eyelids as she stared out the window, and his heart panged with compassion.

Truth was, he hadn't exactly been friendly to the woman. She'd seemed nice enough. And maybe that was part of the reason he'd chosen not to speak and had only nodded curt greetings in passing.

Getting close to people—and then losing them—was so hard. It was beyond hard.

It was heartbreaking.

Images of Grace and Willow filled his thoughts again, and a radiating pain began in his chest. What he wouldn't give to have them beside him again. If he could go back and change time…

But that was just wishful thinking that would get him nowhere.

"Thanks for doing this," Sienna murmured. She pulled her sweater tighter and glanced away from the window a moment.

The somberness in her gaze spoke volumes. Tonight had shaken her to the core, yet she'd still remained graceful and kind. His respect for the woman grew.

"It's not a problem." Devin stole another glance at her and saw her exhaustion. "I know you've been through this with the police, but could you tell me what you know about Anita?"

Detective Jenson had told them that Anita Gwinn didn't exist until four months ago. That had just been a preliminary finding, of course. The police would contact the school system and find her records there. They'd track down her Social Security number. There was still a good chance that the woman was real and did exist. It was too early to say.

Sienna let out a heavy breath, as if carrying the burdens of the world. And, in a way, she was. She was carrying the burdens of Colby's world, at least.

"I wish I knew more," she started, her voice soft and almost fragile. "I really do. But I only worked with Anita for a few months. She'd just moved here from Arizona. I had the impression she was leaving a bad situation. Maybe an abusive husband or boyfriend? She didn't like to talk about it."

"You said there's no father in the picture?" He glanced in his rearview mirror and saw the headlights behind him.

Was it someone following them? Or was it just

another traveler headed the same way? Devin hoped it was the latter. Prayed it was.

"By all indications, there is no father," Sienna said, clueless about the potential danger on their heels.

Devin would keep it that way for as long as he could. The woman had already been through a lot. And there was no need to alarm her for no reason.

He drew his gaze away from the rearview mirror as they climbed higher and the road became narrower. "Where did her mom live? You said her mother was having surgery?"

"Anita told me her mom was out in Kansas. I didn't ask questions. Figured Anita didn't have a reason to lie to me. And maybe she didn't lie. Maybe she's a victim here or she was in a car accident or… I really don't know what to think." Sienna swung her head back and forth, her features pinched with anxiety. "Maybe all of this is a misunderstanding."

She didn't sound like she believed that any more than Devin did.

Devin had the urge to reach over and offer his neighbor some kind of comfort. But he didn't. It…didn't seem appropriate and, though this wasn't an official assignment, he wanted to keep things on the up-and-up. Still, his heart hurt for the woman and her distress.

A stranger had turned her life upside down.

Silence fell between them, and the sweet sound of Colby snoozing filled the car.

Devin glanced in the mirror again. The lights were still there behind him on the road. No one else followed, just the one lone car. Most people weren't out on the road at 3:00 a.m.

He needed to figure out if he was being followed once and for all.

As he came up on a street, he veered to the left.

"What…?" Sienna muttered, her eyes widening.

Devin kept his grip tight on the steering wheel. *Keeping a cool head means keeping everyone alive.* That's what one of his instructors at Quantico had always said. That was what Devin needed to adhere to now as well.

"Sorry," he muttered. "I'm taking a little detour."

Sienna craned her neck behind her as the truth seemed to click in her mind. "Are we being followed?"

"I didn't say that."

Her gaze was sharp as she turned to him. "You didn't deny it, either."

"I'm just being cautious." And the woman was no dummy. That was good, because they'd need to keep their wits about them to get through this situation.

The way Sienna squeezed the armrest didn't

go unnoticed, nor did the way she rubbed her forehead with her other hand. "I just don't understand."

"I don't think any of us do." He kept his eyes on the narrow road as the asphalt edged closer to the mountain's edge.

"Is this about me? Colby? Anita?"

"Until we have more information, we won't know." Another glance in the rearview mirror showed that the car had turned also. They were definitely being followed.

The driver didn't appear to be aggressive. That was the good news. The bad news was that he—or she—wasn't backing off, either. Devin tried to get a better look at the vehicle, to see if it was the same one he'd seen earlier—the one the intruder had jumped into. It was too dark to tell, but that was his suspicion.

"What are we going to do?" Sienna asked, glancing over her shoulder again.

"We're going to have to lose them."

She sucked in a quick breath. "But…these are back roads. Mountainous. There aren't a lot of places to go."

So she was familiar was this area. And she was correct. These were winding, narrow streets where one wrong move could mean crashing into a mountain or going off a cliff.

Neither of those things were options. Devin was going to have to do his best in the situation.

The one thing he wouldn't be doing was leading the guy straight to his cabin.

Sienna couldn't shake the bad feeling—and rightfully so. Her instincts screamed that danger was on their tail. But it was like she'd just asked Devin: Why? It just didn't make sense. How could the simple task of watching a co-worker's son have turned into this nightmare? This fight for survival?

And now someone was following them. How far was this person going to take it?

Sienna glanced in the back seat at little Colby. He was such a cute kid with his spiky, fine blond hair and cherublike features. He had incredibly long eyelashes that made his blue eyes look even bigger than they already were. His favorite word was *more*, and he could entertain himself for hours just playing with pots and pans.

He snoozed in his car seat, unaware of anything going on around him. What Sienna wouldn't give to have that kind of peace and serenity in the midst of a storm like this.

Her life hadn't worked out according to plan.

She wasn't supposed to be here in Colorado. She wasn't supposed to be single without children.

But she was. And on most days, she made the best of it.

But right now, all Sienna felt was resentment. And fear. A lot of fear.

"Hold on." Devin turned the wheel sharply again.

Sienna held her breath as they pulled onto another mountain road—this one smaller, tighter, possibly more winding. As the SUV turned, she reached for the armrest, grabbing Devin's hand instead. She quickly pulled away as she felt a jolt of electricity rush through her.

Electricity? No, that couldn't be right. When—and if—she decided to fall for another man, it would not be someone like Devin. She needed someone warm and friendly.

Then again, her ex, Jackson, had been Mr. Personality, and look where that had gotten her. Humiliated at the altar.

She glanced over at Devin quickly, noting his strong jaw and determined gaze. There was no question the man was attractive and fit. Sienna's friend Viviana used to joke, asking Sienna to call her next time Devin was outside cutting his grass in the heat. The man had light brown hair that was pushed back from his face and a barely-there beard. He towered at least a foot taller than her own five foot three inches.

She closed her eyes, hoping Devin knew what he was doing. Why had she entrusted her life and Colby's to him? What had she been thinking? That hotel room was looking better and better all the time. Yet Devin seemed so confident and protective. Maybe in a subconscious way she'd been drawn to that.

Being alone out here in Colorado—being single—it wasn't easy. Most of the time she prided herself on being independent. But deep inside, it would be nice to have someone watching out for her. Never in her wildest dreams had she thought it would be Devin.

Sienna had only said yes because she knew Devin was FBI. She'd seen him talking with the officers on the scene. He'd seemed respected and professional. He'd also been surprisingly kind.

She gripped the armrest as she glanced out the window and saw the steep cliff beside her. She wasn't sure she'd be able to breathe until they reached the end of this. Until the car was no longer behind them.

This whole thing was a bad idea. She *should* have gotten that hotel room and begged the police to station a guard outside it.

Why hadn't she thought of that an hour ago?

Instead, she was in the middle of the wild, rugged mountains with a man who was virtually a stranger. If this car hit them, they'd have no help. There would be nowhere to go.

This was all a bad, bad idea.

"It's going to be okay," Devin said.

Sienna wished she felt as certain as he sounded. Because nothing felt okay right now.

She could hardly move, much less turn her head. "Is he still there?"

Devin's eyes flickered into the rearview mirror. "I don't see him yet."

"Do you know where this road goes?"

"It goes to the top of the mountain."

"To your cabin?"

"No."

"Then where?

"It ends."

Sienna sucked in a breath. "That doesn't sound like a great plan."

"Trust me."

"I hardly know you."

"I realize that. And I know this is difficult. But I do have a plan." With that, Devin turned the wheel again—turned it hard again—until they barreled toward some tall pine trees on the edge of the road.

Sienna sucked in a breath when she spotted the blackness just beyond the trees. It was dark there because there was nothing. Nothing but a cliff.

Just what was Devin thinking? He was going to kill them all.

Sienna's racing heart agreed.

As the edge of the cliff got closer and closer, a small voice came from the back seat. "Mama? Mama?"

Colby was awake. And he began to wail in fear.

The sound echoed in the car, matching exactly what Sienna was feeling.

Especially when, in the next instant, the SUV lurched forward.

FOUR

Devin watched as the cliff materialized in front of them as a void, as nothing but darkness and air.

Darkness and air that they barreled toward.

Sienna screamed beside Devin and reached for the dash, bracing herself for the impact—or lack thereof.

Devin jerked the steering wheel to the left, and the car drifted.

Devin held his breath.

Waited.

Anticipated.

Finally, the wheels gained traction—only mere inches from the ledge. Just inches beyond that, the earth ended and anything crossing its path would tumble down hundreds of feet.

It could have been a certain death.

Instead, the SUV turned against the rocky road.

Devin released the air in his lungs as the tires

gained traction again. Pressing the accelerator, he sped down a service road running alongside the cliff.

He glanced over at Sienna and saw her pale face. Saw her clutching the armrest. Saw her frozen, hardly even breathing as she stared straight ahead with wide, fear-stricken eyes.

As soon as Colby wailed again, her stupor cracked, and she turned toward the boy. She sounded stiff as she said, "It's going to be okay, sweetie."

Devin glanced in the rearview mirror. The car pursuing them had turned, chasing after him.

He watched as the driver cluelessly charged toward the cliff.

A flash of red lit against the underbrush.

Brake lights.

He vaguely saw the outline of the car. The vehicle still appeared on land—but barely. It had stopped face-first on the rocky ledge.

His heart rate slowed. That would slow this guy down for a while. He'd have to carefully maneuver the vehicle out—which would buy Devin some much-needed time.

Devin continued down the road until turning right back onto the street he'd originally been traveling on. But instead of heading in the same direction, he decided to take the longer way around—just to ensure this guy didn't get a clue about where he was going.

"What are you doing?" Sienna asked. Fear laced her voice—and maybe a touch of weariness.

"I'm just taking an alternate route. I don't want to lead this guy to the cabin."

"This place…could he look it up under your name?"

Good. She was thinking things through. That was what they needed right now—to keep a cool ahead. "It's in my uncle's name—on my mom's side. This guy shouldn't find it. If he does, it's going to take some time. We'll be safe there for tonight, at least."

Colby wailed in the back again.

Devin saw the tension across Sienna's face. Not being able to hold the child now was killing her. She angled her body toward the back seat and extended her hand. The boy latched on to her finger instead.

Devin wished he could stop and let Sienna hold Colby now, but they couldn't risk the interruption. No, right now they needed to get as far away as possible. Time was of the essence, especially until they were safe and out of sight.

Thankfully, the cabin was only a couple miles from here.

Devin's knuckles were white as he gripped the steering wheel. There was more going on here than he'd ever assumed, and he didn't like any of it. There were too many unknowns. Too much danger. Too much at stake.

Namely, Colby. By default, Sienna as well. The lengths this guy was going to showed desperation and determination.

Finally, Devin reached his old family cabin. It was set off far from the road, nestled in a fortress of tall trees and mountains. The nine-hundred-square-foot log home with the broad porch was a welcome sight.

The place brought back a flash of memories—some warm, others grief stricken. He didn't have time to dwell on the past now, though. No, right now was about survival.

He pulled the car around to the back, just in case their pursuer drove past. He wanted to make it as difficult as possible for anyone to locate them, and he'd take every precaution necessary.

"This is it?" Sienna asked, staring out the window.

"This is it. Let's get Colby out of here."

She nodded and scrambled into action. A few minutes later, she had Colby in her arms and bounced him up and down while murmuring in the boy's ear. The child calmed down as soon as she held him.

The sight of them together made his heart ache and brought back memories—memories that were always too close to the surface. He shoved them aside, not having time to deal with them now—even if they wanted to batter him into submission.

Still, Devin would feel better once they were inside and they had some answers. He grabbed the few bags they'd had time to pack and ushered the two people he'd vowed to protect into the cabin.

Sienna breathed a sigh of relief as Colby finally closed his eyes. His breathing evened out, signaling he'd fallen asleep. After arriving at the cabin, she'd held him in her arms, singing soft songs and rocking him in a stiff wooden rocking chair in the corner of a dark guest bedroom.

She'd thought the boy would never go to sleep—and she couldn't blame him after the events of this evening. She wasn't sure she would be able to sleep, either, with everything on her mind.

When she was sure Colby was out, Sienna carefully placed the child in a bed that Devin had shoved against the wall. She pulled a blanket up over him and placed several pillows on the edge of the bed, just so he wouldn't roll off.

When she was satisfied Colby was safe and secure, she stepped out of the bedroom. The rest of the cabin was still bathed in darkness as well, but her eyes had mostly adjusted. She spotted Devin standing guard by the front window, his face a mere silhouette.

Her gaze scanned the rest of the cabin. She hadn't had time to look much when she'd arrived.

It was small—a great room with three bedrooms branching out around the perimeter. In typical cabin fashion, leather furniture decorated the space, along with plaid curtains and three stuffed deer heads on the wall. The place smelled partly like dust and partly like a pine forest.

Under other circumstances, Sienna might actually enjoy being here in nature.

But not knowing what she did—knowing what was at stake and the lengths the unknown man would go to to get what he wanted.

She shivered as a chill washed over her.

"I would start a fire, but I don't want to draw attention to the cabin," Devin said, turning away from the window and stepping toward him.

"Probably smart." She lowered herself on the couch across from him.

"Here's a blanket." He picked up one folded beside him and handed it to her. "It should stave off the cold some."

She took the fleece from him and wrapped it over her shoulders. "You think we'll be safe here?"

Devin frowned—not the most reassuring reaction she could hope for. But at least the man was being honest and realistic. He sat down on the couch across from her.

"For tonight, at least," he said.

"That man will keep trying to find us." Sienna's voice trembled as she remembered the terror she'd felt earlier. Flashbacks hit her. Flashbacks of facing down the intruder. Having a gun held at her head. It would take her a long time to move past that and not panic at every creak in the night that she heard.

"I know."

"I just don't understand why." She was thinking aloud, she supposed. It was just that nothing made sense. But she didn't expect Devin to have answers.

Frankly, she was surprised he was even involved. Not *only* was Devin involved, he was *deeply* involved at this point. He could have lost his life just as easily as her and Colby when that car was chasing them earlier.

"Nothing else came to mind now that some of the initial shock has worn off?" Devin leaned forward with his elbows propped against his legs.

"I'm not sure the initial shock has worn off." She pulled the blanket closer—not because she needed to feel warm. No, because she needed to feel safe. "And, no. Nothing else has come to mind. I'm clueless about all of this. Clueless about where Anita is and why she's not answering her phone. Who that man was. Why he would want Colby."

"I know the police are working on it. Hopefully they'll figure out some answers soon and everything will return to normal."

That was right. Maybe in the morning this nightmare would be over and Sienna could resume her life. Go back to teaching her precious little kindergarteners. Taking walks in the park with Colby. Watching her favorite movies as she drifted off to sleep.

For some reason, she doubted that was true, though. Her gut told her this ordeal was a long way from being finished. And, even when it was, her life would never be quite the same.

Hopefully, her gut was wrong.

Just then, her phone rang. She felt the blood drain from her face as she shuffled through her purse to find the device.

"I don't recognize the number," she muttered, glancing up at Devin.

Devin crossed the space between them and lowered himself beside her. He glanced at the screen. "Answer anyway. Put it on speaker."

Sienna's hands trembled as she accepted the call. "Hello?"

"I'm coming for you," a man whispered. "Next time, you're going to die."

The words echoed in the room until a sick feeling began to churn in Sienna's stomach.

What did those words—that threat—even mean? And who was this man who was coming for Sienna?

FIVE

Devin grabbed the phone from Sienna, slid the back off and took the battery out. He knew time was of the essence, and they couldn't risk being followed.

"Why'd you do that?" Sienna asked, her mouth dropping open slightly.

"Just in case someone tries to track your number," he said. "It's unlikely, but it's possible. I'm not sure how high-tech these people are, but, until we know more, we shouldn't take any chances."

She shivered, and the slightly offended look in her eyes disappeared. "Good point. The last thing I want to do is lead this man right to us."

Devin heard the concern in her voice, and his heart panged with compassion. "I'm going to keep an eye on you guys, Sienna."

She didn't seem to hear him.

"I knew he wanted Colby, but he wants to kill me?" She shivered again. "I just… I don't understand."

Devin resisted the urge to touch Sienna's arm or to put his hand on her back. It was tempting, and she looked like she needed comfort. But it wasn't his place. No, he would keep her and Colby safe, but that was all.

"You should try and get some rest," he encouraged her.

"I wish I could. But I'm certain I can't. My brain is working overtime."

"Maybe I can find something to make some coffee with, then." He stood.

Thankfully, power was still connected to the place. It would just take a while for it to heat up sufficiently. And turning the lights on seemed too dangerous, a surefire signal to anyone going past that they were here. They couldn't take the risk.

"Coffee sounds good." She pulled her sleeves over her hands, making her look more like a college student than a teacher.

Devin made his way into the kitchen and found what he needed. A few minutes later, the pot percolated. Once it was done, he brought two cups over—one for himself and one for Sienna.

He handed Sienna hers. "Sorry—no cream or sugar. But it's warm."

"Thank you."

He sat across from her again, his thoughts spinning toward the unknown future. "You said you brought something for Colby to eat in the morning, correct?"

"Yes, that's correct. I grabbed some of his favorite snacks and some juice, cereal and bananas before we left."

"Good, at least we don't have to worry about that." He had so many other things on his mind—food wasn't at the top of his list. He and Sienna could make do with whatever they found, but not the baby.

He glanced up as he felt Sienna studying him.

"Why are you helping us, Devin?" she asked, not looking the least bit embarrassed or apologetic to be caught staring. "Why put your own life at risk?"

"I wouldn't be able to live with myself if I sat back while something happened to you."

"But you don't even know us." Confusion stretched through her voice.

"I don't have to know you. I know enough. You're a single woman and Colby is a child. I can't leave you on your own with someone trying to kill you."

She held her coffee in front of her with both hands, ready to take a sip. "Well, that's really nice of you. I just hope you don't regret it. I'm not sure what lies ahead."

"None of us do, do we?" Devin's voice caught. His whole life had been proof that what a person hoped waited for them in the future was often not reality.

Sienna took a sip of her coffee and leaned back. "No, we don't. Funny how we've lived beside each other for six months and this is the most we've ever spoken."

If Devin was smart, he wouldn't be too chatty now, either. Sienna did look so inviting, though, with that black-and-red flannel blanket around her and with her fingers hugging that coffee mug.

Maybe that was why he'd always stayed away from her, for that matter. Because Sienna was inviting, and he didn't want to tempt himself.

His heart would always belong to his wife. To even entertain the idea of giving his love to someone else felt like a betrayal. So his walls went up. And they stayed up. It was all he knew to do.

Devin needed to make sure those walls stayed stronger than ever. Because the peril around them could test all of his limits.

Sienna took another sip of her coffee, her mind racing. She hated just sitting here and waiting. Hated the questions fluttering in her mind. There had to be something she could do—something besides thinking about the turbulence in Devin's gaze and the haunted look in his eyes.

She swallowed hard and pushed down the questions about her handsome neighbor. She had other much more pressing things she needed to consider and figure out. The sooner they had answers, the sooner she could resume her life.

"Devin, is there a computer here?" she finally asked.

"There's one in the corner. Why?"

"Do you mind if I use it? I'd like to do my own research on Anita."

"I suppose it can't hurt." He stood and directed her to an old desktop. "We'll have to use my hot spot to log in. No internet here."

"I should have guessed."

Sienna sat there, her fingers poised to begin typing. As she hit a key, the computer came to life. The glow from the screen cast its light in the room.

Devin didn't move from his spot beside her, peering at the screen in curiosity.

And something about his nearness had Sienna's nerves on edge.

It was the situation, she told herself. And that was all.

After getting signed on to Devin's hot spot, she typed Anita's name into the search engine. A little ball formed on the screen, letting Sienna know it was going to take a moment to get her results. Sienna couldn't help but muse at the complete silence around her.

At home, she could hear the air blowing through her vents as the HVAC either chilled or heated her house. Could hear the hum of the lights. The swish of the dishwasher. Cars passing by on a nearby highway.

Here…there was so much stillness that it was almost unnerving.

The wind blew a spattering of debris against the cabin just then, breaking up the tension that had begun to stretch across her shoulders. She hoped that was the only unexpected sound she heard tonight. No more windows being shoved open or unexpected footfalls or the click of a gun being cocked.

Finally, the little ball on the screen disappeared, and results were listed down the page.

It was like Detective Jenson said. Anita's social media account didn't appear until four months ago. But Sienna herself hadn't opened an account until six months ago. Social media just wasn't her thing.

Sienna clicked on the woman's profile picture and studied it a moment. Anita was petite—probably just over five feet—and twenty pounds or so overweight. She had blond hair that was cut to her shoulders in no particular style. She hardly ever wore makeup, but she did wear a necklace with a crown trinket at the end.

Sienna had asked her once if there was any significance to the jewelry, but Anita had told Sienna that she just liked the piece.

There were no pictures of Anita with Colby,

nor did her profile share very much information other than the fact she liked ice cream with caramel on top, she loved working with children and she was born in September.

Why were there no pictures of her with Colby? Someone as bubbly as Anita should thrive on social media. And the woman was always snapping pictures on her phone. She insisted on showing them to everyone when she got to school each day. It wasn't a bad thing. But even when Sienna was in a hurry, Anita didn't seem to notice. She had all the time in the world.

"It just doesn't make sense," Sienna muttered, leaning back in the rickety computer chair.

Devin shifted beside her. "Maybe she doesn't like being online."

Sienna shook her head. "Anita seems like the type to love stuff like this. I just can't believe she had nothing until she moved to this area. She was the type of person who would insert herself into conversations when she wasn't welcome. She was clueless about it. Or she'd interrupt you to tell you something new that Colby had done. She had one of those grating personalities where everything was all about her."

"It sounds suspicious that she doesn't have a more flourishing social media presence then, doesn't it? People that like attention seem to thrive on social media."

Sienna twisted in her chair to better face

Devin and see his expression. "Why would she move here and create a new identity?"

"Maybe she's running from something. Maybe an abusive ex-husband?"

Sienna's heart ached with a jab of grief—grief that quickly mingled with excitement. Maybe Devin was on to something. She'd considered that possibility before but what if this was much more serious than she'd allowed herself to believe?

"Maybe that is what happened," Sienna said. "Maybe she left him, and now he's trying to get Colby back."

"I'll make sure the police look into it. But that could be a decent lead."

Just then, she turned and their knees brushed. Another jolt of electricity traveled through her, and she let out a gasp and quickly pulled back.

She hadn't expected that. Not at all.

And she didn't welcome it happening again, either. Whenever she did decide she was interested in dating again, it would not be with a man like Devin. No, it wouldn't be with someone who was brooding and cranky and unfriendly. She needed someone who was relaxed. Laid-back. Kind.

The first jolt of electricity had just been an accident. A misunderstanding between her brain and her heart. But for it to happen twice? That wasn't good.

She cleared her throat, embarrassed by her reaction. "Until we learn Anita's real identity, we won't know if the theory—that she's running from someone—is correct, though."

"Don't you have to be fingerprinted to work at the school?"

Sienna nodded. "That's right. They could trace her fingerprints."

"But only if she has a criminal record."

Her excitement died just as quickly as it had risen. "It's true. It's a good thing I'm not in law enforcement, because I'm all out of other ideas."

Devin squeezed her arm. "I know the police are on it right now. Let them worry about it. You should get your rest. Tomorrow could be a long day."

She nodded, feeling a wave of exhaustion come over her. If it was just Sienna taking care of herself, it would be different. But chasing after a twenty-four-month-old was no easy task. It required energy and focus. "You're right. I should. I'm going to need my energy to take care of Colby."

"You can take the other twin bed in his room." Devin stood.

"That sounds great. That way I can keep an eye on him."

"I'll see you in the morning, then."

Reluctantly, she stepped away from Devin. Strange, she thought, how she instantly felt more exposed. She hadn't realized it until this instant, but something about Devin's presence had made her feel safe. He had that bodyguard type of presence. It felt good to know someone was watching her back. Protecting her.

But she had a child to care for. She didn't have time to worry about her own feelings or fears. No, she had to keep Colby away from the man who'd broken into her house.

And she would.

If it was the last thing she did.

Devin paced the wooden floor of the cabin. He couldn't sleep. No, he wouldn't let himself. He needed to stay awake. To listen.

Whoever had followed them had been clearly desperate. Desperate people wouldn't stop just because their car was hanging off a cliff. No, as soon as that driver got his car back in order, he would keep looking. Or, even worse, maybe he was working with someone.

Either way, Devin couldn't rest. His adrenaline still pumped through him, and his thoughts raced.

If someone was determined enough, he could hit each of the side streets leading up this mountain. If he did that, he would eventually find this cabin.

Devin didn't want to think like that, but he

had to be prudent. He had to face the fact that it was a possibility.

If worse came to worst, he could bring someone else in to help them. He hoped it didn't come to that, though. He preferred keeping his circle small, especially in situations like this. The fewer people who knew where they were, the better.

He chewed on the theory about Anita having an abusive ex. It could be plausible. What if Colby's father was trying to get him back and would stop at nothing to do just that? It made sense, and it was the most plausible excuse he could think of.

Devin called Detective Jenson and ran the theory past him.

"That's an interesting idea," Jenson said. "I'll look into it. But until we know this woman's real identity, I'm not sure we can prove any of it."

"Any headway in that area?"

"We're running her fingerprints and photo through one of our programs. We've also sent a team to her house to see if we can find anything there. So far, there's nothing."

"That's unfortunate."

"Whoever she really is, she was careful to conceal her true identity."

"She's either smart or desperate."

"Maybe both."

"Maybe both," Devin conceded.

After Devin ended the call, he stepped toward the window and peered outside.

Darkness stared back. A good acre of trees stood between the cabin and the road. The lane snaking through the woods to the cabin was concealed by the forest, so unless someone was looking for the entry to the place, a person could pass it.

Devin had a lot of great memories of coming here as a child. Memories of hiking through the mighty pine forests surrounding the mountains. Of fishing with his dad at the creek that was only a short walk away. Of taking their catches of the day and grilling out on the back deck. His mom would make her grilled corn salad. They'd play games outside and just enjoy each other's company.

Family time. He remembered that far more than he remembered the birthday gifts he'd received.

He also remembered bringing Grace and Willow here. He'd wanted to share the memories with them, though Grace had been more of a city girl. He'd been hoping she'd warm up to the idea of a cabin life, but it had felt too much like camping to her.

Still, this was the place where a person could find peace. Could he say the same when all of this was over? He didn't know.

Devin paused as something in the distance caught his eye.

Was that light between the trees?

Devin sucked in a breath.

He squinted.

A flashlight? Coming through the woods?

No, Devin realized. It was the distant headlights of a car passing on the lane.

He tensed. It could just be someone traveling through the area. Or it could be the person who was looking for them.

He pulled the gun from his shoulder holster and waited.

Another set of lights went past.

Two cars in five minutes? Or was it someone who'd driven past, missed the lane and turned around to come back and check it out?

His mind raced through possibilities. Should he wake Sienna and Colby and run? Or stand his ground?

Right now, his bets were on standing his ground. Until he knew if he was overreacting, he had to keep a cool head.

He continued to wait, looking for another glimmer of illumination through the foliage outside the cabin.

He saw nothing.

But he didn't let down his guard. Not yet. Because he knew there was a chance the driver had cut his lights. That he was traveling by foot.

And, if he was, Devin would be ready and on guard when he arrived.

SIX

Sienna awoke with a start. She sat up straight in bed, saw the strange surroundings, and in an instant, everything flashed back to her.

The man who'd broken into her house. Fleeing. Being followed. Coming to this strange cabin with her aloof neighbor.

She glanced over at the other twin bed across the room. Quickly, she pulled her blanket back and rushed toward Colby. She released the breath she held.

He was sleeping soundly. The boy had always been a good sleeper—a fact she was grateful for right now. And even better, he didn't seem any worse for wear after everything that had happened yesterday.

Glancing at the time, she saw that it was six thirty. Early-morning sunlight was already trickling in through the trees. She needed to borrow Devin's phone and call in to her school, let them know she wouldn't be there today. Even though it was June, she taught at a small private school that had a year-round schedule.

She lumbered into the living room, pausing in the doorway as she spotted Devin standing by the window, a steaming cup of coffee in his hands. He'd changed clothes—he'd brought an overnight bag with him. He'd donned clean jeans and a black T-shirt. His dark hair looked combed and his skin clean.

He turned when he heard her footsteps and offered a tight smile. "Morning."

"Morning. How did it go last night?" Sienna pushed her hair from eyes.

An unreadable emotion crossed Devin's gaze, and he turned his back from the window and stepped closer. "It was okay."

What wasn't he telling her? Sienna felt certain there was something.

Yet here they all were. Safe. In one piece.

Maybe in good time Devin would share whatever worry was on his mind.

"Did you get any sleep?" Sienna leaned against the doorjamb and ignored the thought that wanted to materialize in her mind. The thought that this conversation could really be awkward considering the fact that the two of them hardly knew each other.

"No, not yet. There will be time for that later."

That didn't sound healthy. In fact, it even

sounded contrary to Devin's own advice to her last night. But she didn't bring that up. Not now.

"May I use your phone to call in to work? I also need to call my best friend. She'll have search parties out for me otherwise."

"Of course. Just don't give away our location." He handed her his phone. "But I'm sure you know that."

Sienna made her calls and returned the phone to Devin, who handed her a protein bar and a cup of coffee.

"I thought you might need this," he said.

Her stomach rumbled at the thought of eating. She hadn't realized she was hungry, but she was. "I do. Thank you."

She sat at the dining room table, Devin taking a seat across from her. Based on his stiff body language, he wasn't sitting to be social. No, he had something on his mind, which was fine, because Sienna had a lot on her mind also.

"Do we have a plan for today?" She took the wrapper off the protein bar and listened to it crinkle before taking a bite of the peanut butter–flavored breakfast. It wasn't the best she'd ever had, but it was nourishment. It was nothing a cup of coffee couldn't wash down.

"We're going to lie low for a while longer," Devin said, taking another sip of his own coffee. "I'm trying to set up a secondary location where we can go, if we need to."

"And by 'if we need to,' you mean, if we need to because we're discovered?"

He shrugged. "I need to stay ahead of this. But I realize that running is difficult with Colby."

It was difficult. Colby needed stability. But in order for him to have stability, maybe they couldn't stay here. His safety trumped everything else right now.

"How long do we have here?" she asked.

"I don't know. As soon as you're done eating, why don't you get cleaned up? Keep your stuff together. We have to be prepared to move, if it comes to it."

Any enjoyment she'd gotten out of the coffee disappeared. This wasn't a quick trip to the mountains until everything blew over. No, this was a life-or-death situation, and she'd be wise to remember it.

An hour later, Sienna was dressed in some clean clothes she'd brought with her. Colby had woken up. She'd gotten him fed and dressed as well. The boy seemed clueless about everything going on around them—which was a blessing.

Sienna couldn't stop thinking about it all. She'd tried to entertain Colby with some songs and by playing patty-cake, but the emotional toll was beginning to take effect on her. She was exhausted, and Colby wasn't.

"Here, buddy. Check these out." Devin squatted on the floor and pulled something from a bookshelf.

Sienna watched carefully. Devin held little wooden cars, probably handmade. And they looked older, like something Devin might have played with himself as a boy.

Colby looked timidly at Devin a moment before reaching for one. Devin handed it to him, his face taking on a different demeanor. Gone was the law enforcement professional. In his place was more of a fatherly figure.

The sight gripped Sienna's heart. She had no idea Devin could have a soft, nurturing side. Something about it melted her insides just a little. Her ex had been like the pied piper—he could attract people faster than anyone she'd ever met before. But most of those relationships only went skin deep. They were a flash in the pan, ending as quickly as they'd begun.

Devin played with Colby for several minutes, making funny car sounds on the floor and driving the vehicles over imaginary hills.

Colby loved it.

After a few minutes, Devin stood and came back over to her. There was a strange look in his eyes.

Was that grief?

No, that couldn't be right.

Or maybe it was. There was so much Sienna didn't know about the man.

And none of it was her business, either.

"Do you mind?" She nodded to the computer.

"Go right ahead. Just be careful—don't share your location, either purposefully or accidentally. And I'm not saying you're that ignorant. I'm only saying that you'd be surprised how many people do just that."

"I'll be careful." Sienna logged in to her social media account. She'd only gotten a profile at all because everyone in her grade level had decided to start a group chat there together. She hadn't checked her pages in months, though.

She wasn't sure what she hoped she might find here. Maybe an update from her friends at school. Maybe they had heard something, especially when Sienna hadn't shown up at work this morning.

She needed some kind of connection to her regular life right now, and social media seemed as good a choice as anything.

She did have a couple messages from her colleagues. One said she hoped Sienna was doing okay and that she missed seeing her today. The second was from her assistant, who said the kids had made her a card.

They must think she was sick or that Colby wasn't feeling well. That was a more likely scenario than the implausible situation she'd found herself in.

Just before she was going to close out of the

site and return to the mindless task of fretting, a new message popped up.

Sienna's breath caught. "Devin, it's from Anita."

He rushed toward her.

As her eyes scanned the words, her pulse throbbed louder in her ears.

Sienna, I know this is all confusing. I can't explain right now. But please keep Colby safe. And whatever you do, don't trust the police.

She looked up at Devin. "What does this mean?"

His grim face said it all. "I don't know. But I don't like it."

Devin leaned over the computer. "Type back. Ask Anita where she is and if she's okay."

Sienna drew in a deep breath and did as he asked.

Then they both waited. But there was nothing. No response.

Devin knew it was a long shot that Anita would reply. But it was worth a try, and she still might reply eventually.

"Let's keep an eye on it, okay?" Devin said. "Maybe she'll reach out again. The more information we have on the woman, the better."

Sienna nodded, still looking apprehensive. "Did you hear anything about her true identity?"

"No, I haven't heard from any of my contacts yet." He'd called his superior at the FBI and told him what was going on. He wanted to remain on the up-and-up and not test his limits, since he was officially on a sabbatical. His boss had given him clearance to help with the case.

All of that had happened during the wee hours of the morning as he stood watch at the cabin. Nothing had materialized from those lights he'd seen through the trees. Maybe it just had been a car—or two cars—traveling down the mountain road in the distance. Either way, he had to remain careful.

Sienna's gaze went to Colby. "All I can think about is who Anita really is. Why she's running. How this all might affect Colby."

Devin followed her line of sight, grief clutching his heart at the sight of Colby. His daughter used to like to sit in that very place and play with his old toys, as well. Sometimes, it felt like a lifetime ago. Other times, it felt like just yesterday.

How he missed Willow. And he always would. There was a gaping hole in his heart that he was certain would never go away or heal.

Devin cleared his throat. "Hopefully, all of this won't affect Colby. He's young enough that he can bounce back. I doubt he'll remember most of it."

"We need to keep it that way. I can't stomach the thought of someone taking him and what kind of trauma that would place on him. It's not healthy." Sienna crossed her arms, a determined look in her eyes.

Devin appreciated the woman's concern for the boy. Sienna was kind and empathetic—just the kind of person you wanted to watch your child in a jam. Only this one had put her directly in harm's way.

Sienna suddenly stood and let out a long breath, one that showed exhaustion. "I should figure out the food situation. It will be lunchtime soon."

"There's not much here, but I think I saw some cans of tuna fish that haven't expired and some crackers."

"I'll see what I can put together."

"That would be great." Devin didn't argue. It would be good for her to keep her mind occupied. Besides, he wanted to make a phone call.

As Sienna went into the kitchen, and with Colby still occupied and safe, he stepped into a bedroom and pulled out his cell. He dialed Detective Jenson's number.

"Devin, what can I do for you?" Detective Jenson said.

"I was hoping you might be willing to give me an update on the situation." As soon as he said the words, Devin wondered about Anita's warning. *Don't trust the police.* Why would she say that? And whom was she referring to?

He had no idea.

"Not much to share," Detective Jenson said. "We haven't been able to figure out the woman's real identity or even if she's alive."

"She sent a message online to Sienna. Said she was okay, to keep Colby safe and not to trust the police."

Detective Jenson paused for a minute. "That's interesting. Any idea why she would say that?"

"Like I mentioned earlier, I wonder if she's running from the baby's father or an abusive situation. Maybe the baby's father is in law enforcement, for that matter."

"Something to consider," Jenson said. "In the meantime, you want to give me a location? In case we need to find you?"

Devin thought about his response before saying, "The less people who know, the better." Even more so now that Anita had posted her warning.

"Okay then. It's your call. But if you need us, we won't know how to find you."

It was a risk Devin was willing to take—for now, at least. "You just do your job, and I'll worry about keeping them safe."

"Very well. I hope you're not making a mistake, though."

Me too, he thought. *Me too.*

Just as Devin ended the call, a sound sliced through the air.

His back muscles clenched as his body instantly reacted. He grabbed his gun.

That was a bullet.

Someone was firing at the cabin.

SEVEN

Sienna felt something whiz by her, and she sucked in a quick breath.

Was that a…?

Before the thought could fully form, Devin sprinted from the bedroom, his gun drawn. "Get down!"

She ran toward Colby and threw herself over the child on the floor.

A bullet, she realized.

Someone had shot at her and come inches from hitting her.

Her heart raced out of control.

Colby let out a cry and reached out his arms around her neck, clinging to her. Sienna clung back, praying that he wouldn't be hurt.

Please, Lord, spare this child. He doesn't deserve all of this. Protect him.

She found comfort in the realization that whoever was coming after them probably didn't want to hurt Colby. But this man, no doubt, would kill Sienna in order to take Colby.

She squeezed her eyes shut at the thought.

Something touched her shoulder. A hand. Devin's hand.

"Are you okay?" he asked, urgency on his face as he stood there with his gun drawn.

She nodded, not really sure if she was okay or not.

"Stay here," he ordered.

A knot formed in her throat as she watched Devin dart toward the opposite wall—the direction from which the bullet had come. What if the shooter killed Devin as he tried to protect her and Colby? She could hardly stomach the thought.

Put Your hedge of protection around Devin, too, Father. Please end this madness.

How had Sienna's life felt so normal just yesterday at this time? Other than being unable to connect with Anita, her life had continued as planned. She'd dropped Colby off at the school's day care. She'd gone to work. Picked up Colby. Gone to dinner with Viviana at a Mexican place they'd been wanting to try out. Colby had loved munching on the free chips and had eaten an entire chicken quesadilla.

And that was the way she liked it. Sienna loved routine and schedules.

Now everything had been shaken.

Colby let out another cry, his little two-year-old mind obviously sensing that danger was near.

"It's going to be okay," she whispered.

He buried his head in the crook of her neck and squeezed her harder.

Maybe this was a fluke. A hunter with bad aim.

But as soon as the thought had entered her mind, another bullet cut through the wall.

Sienna sucked back a scream, unsure how this would all end.

And that thought left her feeling off balance.

Devin peered around the edge of the window, his gun drawn.

Who was out there? And just what were they planning?

Would they stand down? Or shoot until someone died?

That wasn't acceptable.

Devin's gaze scanned the woods behind the house. He saw the tall pine trees. The rocky boulders. A swatch of yellow wildflowers.

Was that where the gunman was? In these woods? Lingering behind a tree?

That's what Devin would guess.

He'd also guess that the man who'd tried to snatch Colby had been hunting for them all night. Maybe he'd found this location. Seen Devin's car parked behind it and realized this was where they were.

He probably had a scope on his gun now that allowed him to see inside, and he'd spotted them.

But he wasn't a good shot. Otherwise, Sienna would be injured right now—if not worse.

Devin scanned the woods again, and his gaze stopped on a glare in the distance.

There. There he was.

Devin couldn't see a face. No, only a shadow.

And the glare must have come from the scope of the gun.

Colby let out another wail behind him, tightening Devin's nerves even more.

Whoever was doing this should be ashamed. Scaring a child like this should be a crime.

And Devin wouldn't let anything happen to Colby. Not if it was the last thing he did.

He positioned his gun, lining it up with the glare of the scope. He held his breath before releasing it slowly, deliberately.

And then he pulled the trigger and listened as the sound echoed across the mountains.

The glare disappeared.

Had he hit him?

Devin squinted, trying to see better.

The shadow was moving, he realized.

Moving away from the cabin.

"Stay here!" Devin yelled.

"Devin!" Sienna called.

He paused for long enough to glance back at them as they took shelter behind the kitchen counter. His heart lurched with grief for them and what they were going through.

"Be careful," Sienna said. "Please."

He nodded and took off.

He had reservations about leaving Sienna and Colby. But if he left now, he might be able to catch this guy and end this once and for all. That was the best-case scenario.

He stepped outside into the brisk early-summer air, his entire body on alert. Normally, the scent of pines would invigorate him. Right now, it put him on full alert.

Carefully, he kept himself concealed by one of the posts on the porch. He scanned the tree line again.

There! There was the gunman.

The man moved through the woods, going away from the cabin. Around him, birds had stopped chirping.

Devin sprinted from the porch.

Just as he did, another bullet shot through the air, hitting near his feet. His pulse sped, but he kept going.

He reached the area where the man had been hiding and knelt on the ground.

Blood. There was blood here. Not a life-threatening amount, but enough.

Devin had hit the man and injured him. Maybe

not enough to stop him from running, but enough to slow him down.

Devin started through the woods, trying to catch him.

But as he took a step, another shot rang out.

This guy didn't want to be caught.

Devin hunkered down behind a huge, rocky boulder.

Another bullet split into the tree beside him, sending splinters of wood flying through the air.

Devin raised his gun and waited until he spotted the figure clothed in black. When he knew he had the shot, he fired back.

A moan cut through the air.

Devin had hit the man again. If he moved quickly, he could catch him. End this. Get the answers they so desperately sought.

Crouching, he moved from his shelter.

He heard the sound of steps ahead of him. Quickly moving steps.

The man was fleeing.

But before he could make headway, he heard an engine start. His heart rate kicked up a notch, and he took off in a run. Before he reached the man, a door slammed and a car sped away.

Devin took off in a run after it.

But he was too late. The car was gone.

He ran back to the cabin, anxious to check on Sienna and Colby.

He prayed they were okay. He desperately

prayed—more desperately than he had in a long, long time. He couldn't lose someone else entrusted to his care and protection.

Sienna hunkered down behind the breakfast bar, still bouncing Colby in her arms.

Dear Lord, please help us. Protect Devin. Protect us. Help us figure out this mess—and get through it alive.

Colby let out another cry.

"Shh," she whispered. "It's going to be okay, baby boy. It's going to be okay."

But nothing felt okay. Nothing.

Images pummeled her. Images of Devin being shot. Being killed. Of the gunman making his way inside to finish Sienna off before snatching Colby away.

Her heart thumped so hard she could feel it in her throat.

No, she had to stay positive. Had to think the best.

Devin was going to get this guy. They'd get some answers. And this would be over.

Yet she had little hope that was true.

She'd heard the bullets. She'd felt the one that had pierced their fortress—the cabin. Had one of those other bullets hit anyone?

She couldn't stand not knowing.

Why was someone so desperate for this baby? Even if her theory was true and the man behind this was Colby's birth father, why go to such desperate measures? Why not just take it to the court?

Unless the man was so dangerous, he knew he didn't stand a chance there.

She clutched Colby tighter.

The thought hadn't comforted her. Not by any stretch.

As Colby got quiet for a moment, Sienna listened.

She heard nothing.

What was going on out there?

More than anything she wanted to go to the window. To see for herself. To have an inkling of what was coming.

But she couldn't risk it.

The minutes ticked by.

She squeezed her eyes shut and said another prayer. *Please, protect Devin.*

She believed in prayer and how God could change things when His people came before Him. She'd grown up going to church, but her relationship with God had only become real to her in the past year. After Jackson had left her, she'd had no choice but to rely on the fact that God had a better plan for her.

And He had.

Still, she couldn't stand the thought of something happening to Devin because of her. She never should have gotten him involved. Then again, she'd never asked for his help. He'd volunteered it, and she'd hardly been able to say no.

A moment later, she heard the door open.

Her spine tightened.

Who was it? The gunman?

She pulled Colby closer.

Heard a footfall. Labored breathing. A pause.

"Sienna?" someone called.

Her breath caught. Devin. That was Devin... she thought.

A moment later, a shadow appeared over her. She lifted her gaze, almost afraid to see who was there.

Relief flushed through her.

Devin.

It was Devin.

She nearly turned into a puddle right there on the floor.

Before she could, Devin took her elbow and pulled her to her feet.

"You're okay," she muttered.

"I am. But we have to get out of here. Our location has been compromised. Grab Colby's things and let's go."

EIGHT

An hour later, Devin pulled up to another cabin. This one belonged to a longtime family friend, Jim Rogers. Devin had called him and mentioned that he needed to get away for a few days. Jim had seemed more than okay with that.

This cabin was similar to Devin's family's place—it was on a secluded lane, surrounded by trees.

Devin had checked the rearview mirror on the entire drive, but he hadn't seen anyone following him. He hadn't seen hardly anyone behind him at all, for that matter.

Good. That was what they needed. They had to stay one step ahead of whoever was behind this.

He cringed as he thought about the confrontation in the woods.

The man he'd been shooting at had been desperate. He hadn't backed down, not even after being shot.

People who were that desperate would go to any length to get what they wanted.

Even worse, Colby and Sienna were in the crosshairs here. They were the ones with the most to lose—Sienna with her life, and Colby with being snatched away into the unknown.

Just what was this guy planning on doing with Colby? Was he the boy's father, someone who wanted Colby back in his life? Or was there an even darker reason? Maybe this man wasn't related and he wanted Colby for some type of black-market adoption.

There were too many horrible reasons out there why someone would want this precious child. Devin couldn't bear to think about some of them.

Dear God, please place Your hand on this situation. Work in a way that only You can work. Keep Colby safe. Sienna, too. Give me the wisdom to know the best choices to both keep people out of harm and to find the person responsible for this.

He treasured his relationship with God. It had always been there, for as long as he could remember. In fact, his father had run a church for cowboys back in Grand Junction. It had been such a huge part of their home life, and it was the only thing that had carried Devin through the death of his wife and child.

Speaking of Sienna and Colby...they'd both

drifted to sleep on the way here, affording Devin some time of quiet reflection. But he would have to wake them now and get them inside. He couldn't risk having them exposed for any longer than necessary.

He nudged Sienna beside him, and her eyes fluttered open.

Suddenly, she sat up straighter, glancing around frantically.

"It's okay," he told her, keeping his voice calm and soothing. "We're here."

She released her breath and ran a hand through her blond hair. "How could I have fallen asleep?"

"You must be exhausted. There's no shame in that. Besides, you'll need your energy."

She craned her head around to the back seat to check on Colby.

"He fell asleep as well," Devin told her. "No worries."

She swung her head to the windshield and stared out at the cabin. "I've been wanting a mountain getaway since I moved to Colorado. I just never expected it to be like this."

"Good that you can keep your sense of humor." He nodded in front of him. "Let's get inside. I know you have to be hungry. Jim always keeps this place stocked, unlike my family's cabin."

She scrambled out and gently lifted a sleeping Colby from his car seat. The boy lay limp against her chest and shoulder.

Devin's heart pounded with another moment of grief. He remembered his wife holding their daughter like that. It had been such a beautiful sight.

One that would never be recreated. A memory that would never come to life again.

How he missed them. Grace and Willow. He pictured Grace with her bob of dark hair and slender figure. Remembered Willow with her mom's hair—but with curls.

Grace had insisted on naming their daughter Willow. She'd grown up in a house with two willow trees out front. She used to take her books and sit beneath the trees to read and draw and have secret club meetings.

She'd decided when she was ten that she would name her firstborn daughter that. And she had.

Devin smiled at the thought.

But this wasn't the time to get sentimental. Instead, he hurried up the steps, grabbed a spare key from under a flowerpot and unlocked the door.

He quickly scoped the place out before ushering Sienna inside. The interior was chilly—probably too chilly for Colby. It was always so much cooler here in the mountains, even in the summer. He adjusted the thermostat.

Meanwhile, Sienna placed Colby on the couch and found a blanket to place around his sleeping figure. His breath caught as he looked at her. Even with everything that had happened, she looked so lovely with her wheat-colored hair pulled back into a neat ponytail. The long-sleeved baby blue T-shirt she wore gave her an air of innocence, and her jeans showed off her thin figure.

Sienna straightened, her eyes still on the child, and sighed. Her voice sounded wistful as she said, "He looks so peaceful, doesn't he?"

Devin paused beside her. "Yeah, he really does. What I wouldn't give to get some rest like that."

"The worries that can keep us awake at night as adults are hard for a child to comprehend."

"For most children, at least."

"You're right. I work with my fair share of kids who've had to grow up too fast because of the bad hand life has dealt them. I'm hoping Colby won't be one of those children who learn the harsh realities of life too quickly."

"Me, too." He licked his lips. There was so much more he could say. But he wouldn't. Not now. Instead, he started toward the kitchen. "Let's get something to eat. We need to keep up our energy, especially since we don't know what's in store for the next couple of days."

She swung her gaze toward him. "You don't think we'll be safe here?"

"I didn't say that. I'm just saying we need to be on guard."

"Agreed." But her gaze showed that she'd heard the truth and had been reminded about just how dangerous this situation was.

He hadn't meant to alarm her—but she needed to be aware of the facts.

She followed him and peered into the freezer behind him.

"There's some steaks in here," he said. "We can defrost them and maybe cook some of this frozen corn."

"That sounds great," Sienna said. "Maybe I can find some rice or pasta in the cupboard."

"There's some soda in the fridge. Would you like one?"

"I don't normally drink them, but that sounds great right now. Thank you."

He handed her an orange soda, and they began working on preparing lunch together. It seemed so ordinary, so mundane. Yet maybe it was the best thing for them.

"Where did you live before Colorado?" Devin asked as he poured the frozen corn kernels into a pot of salted water.

"Texas," Sienna said, also pulling out a pot and filling it with water. "God's country."

He smiled. "I liken Colorado to the same thing."

"As you should. It's beautiful here."

"What brought you here, if you don't mind me asking?" Why *was* Devin asking? He should keep things simple. Impersonal. Yet the conversation seemed natural, and he had to admit he was curious to know more about the woman.

"No, not at all." Sienna paused at the counter, casually pressing her palms into the laminate top behind her. "I actually moved here to get married."

His eyebrows shot up. That was not what he'd expected to hear. "I had no idea."

"No, it's okay. I gave up my job and moved here so I could get settled before getting married. But my fiancé decided at the altar that marrying me would be the biggest mistake of his life. He called things off."

Devin's heart panged with compassion. "Ouch."

Sienna shrugged, though a sadness passed through her gaze. "It definitely wasn't the best moment of my life. But you know what? I just have to believe that God has something better in mind for me."

Did Sienna believe in God? Devin should have figured. He saw her leaving every Sunday morning, and he'd figured she was headed to church.

He'd only seen her because he'd been headed to church also.

"You decided to stay in Colorado?" he asked.

"I'd already moved here. I already had a job at the school. They'd had the goodbye parties for me at home. I figured, why not? Why not give this place a chance?"

"And?"

"And I like it here," she said. "The people are nice. The mountains are wonderful. At the end of the school year, I'll reevaluate."

"And think about moving back?"

"I'm considering it. I mean, I'm single. I have no family here. I'm slowly making friends. Honestly, I just don't know. But I've been praying."

He hardly knew the woman, but suddenly the thought of her moving away made him feel a new wave of grief. Which was crazy. Because, like he said, he hardly knew her.

Yet he was liking the person he was getting to know more and more.

Sienna was fascinating. Plucky. She had faith that was admirable, and she'd put her life on hold to help a child whose mother was MIA. She didn't even seem to give a second thought to it.

Guilt rose in him. The last thing he needed was to entertain any ideas about this woman.

No, to do so would be a betrayal to Grace. And he'd never do that to her. She was his one and only love.

Devin grabbed the steaks from the microwave where they'd defrosted, ready to start cooking them. If he was smart, he'd stay focused.

Sienna noticed the shift in Devin and wondered why he'd suddenly become colder. The man was always brooding and mysterious—

though incredibly handsome. His light brown hair was tousled. He hadn't shaved, so his cheeks and upper lip had the shadow of a beard. Even though he was only wearing jeans and a black T-shirt, he could have been wearing a tux. It was a good look on him.

But the fact that the man was attractive meant nothing. The last thing she needed was to be interested in someone else. Nope, that hadn't worked out too well for her last time.

Besides, his change of mood didn't matter, she supposed. Maybe she'd been too honest.

But why skirt around the truth? She'd told him what had happened between her and Jackson. She'd left out the details about how heartbroken she'd been. How she'd cried for days. How her family had tried to talk her into leaving Colorado.

Honestly, she'd thought the healthiest thing she could do was to stay put and get herself together. She hadn't expected to fall in love with the area or the people in the area.

She'd met Jackson at a high school football game. She'd traveled an hour from her home to watch her nephew play. Jackson had lived in the area and was at the game to support his alma mater—a school where he'd at one time been the football star and homecoming king.

He'd swept her off her feet, lavishing her with flowers and gifts. He was a lawyer, and he'd done well for himself. He'd been offered a partnership with a firm in Denver.

She'd thought they would have a wonderful life together. And they probably would have.

If Jackson hadn't changed his mind.

But she had to believe that it was for the best and that there were better things ahead. If she didn't believe that, then what hope would she have for the future? Besides, God hadn't let her down yet, and she didn't think He was going to start now.

Besides, Jackson had been impulsive and free-spirited. Too much like her—except when it came to commitment. Sienna believed in keeping her promises.

She stirred the pot full of penne pasta, feeling the steam warm her cheeks until she put the lid back on.

"I guess you grew up here since your family has a cabin in the area," she said, trying to be careful how much she pried. She could sense Devin was a private man, yet she was desperate for small talk. Besides, he'd surprised her—in a good way—and she was curious.

"That's right. I did. Not far from here at least, over in Grand Junction. My dad owns a pretty large ranch out that way."

"Wait, am I hearing that you're actually a cowboy?" She grinned.

He smiled. "Maybe back in the old days I was.

It was a fun way to grow up, but not what I wanted to do forever."

"You managed to get stationed in Denver with the FBI," Sienna said. "I hear that's difficult."

Someone else she'd gone to college with had made it into the FBI, and she knew new agents didn't have much choice where they were assigned, especially when just starting.

"I actually started out in DC." The steaks sizzled on the griddle in front of Devin, and he looked like a natural in the kitchen—another surprise. "But my wife wanted to come back here to family. I was thankful when I was finally able to make that happen."

Sienna's heart pounded in her ears. His wife? So he'd been married. Was he divorced now?

"I see." Sienna bit her tongue so the questions wouldn't pour from her.

Based on the tension of his voice, the subject matter wasn't pleasant.

"Where did you meet your wife?" she heard herself asking.

"At college. We were in the same history class and ended up working together on a project. We were inseparable after that."

Sienna smiled, finding it hard to imagine Devin being head over heels about anyone. No, he seemed too much like a lone ranger. But maybe he hadn't always been like this. Maybe at one time he'd been full of life and love.

Then the proverbial rug had been snatched out from under him.

"Well, it seems like a great place," she finally said. "You been with the FBI for long?"

"Ten years. As you know, I'm on leave right now."

Another mystery. Why was he on leave? What had happened?

"How long is your leave?" She stirred the pasta, letting the steam from the pot warm her face.

"I'm not sure."

Had he messed up? What could have happened?

The man seemed to have everything together—except for the frown he always wore.

"My supervisor didn't like the way I handled a situation," Devin finally said, putting down the tongs he used for the sizzling steak.

"I'm sorry to hear that."

"A drunk driver crashed into a school bus."

"I heard about that." Sienna could hardly breathe as she waited for him to continue. "It happened not long after I moved here."

"I didn't work the case. Drunk drivers aren't FBI jurisdiction. But I happened to drive past the scene right after it happened, and I stopped to help. The supervisor thought I got a little too rough with the driver. I didn't hurt him. I was just trying to scare him, to make him realize the weight of his actions."

"He did almost kill twenty students. If I remember correctly, twelve were taken to the hospital with injuries. And they weren't sure the bus driver was going to make it for a while."

The muscles at his neck tightened. "That's right. He was a repeat offender. He should have known better. But he only cared about himself and getting in one more drink. I've heard the story a million times before."

"It's certainly a tragedy when people get behind the wheel after they have too much alcohol in their system."

"A tragedy describes it well." Devin closed his eyes.

What was going on in his head? Sienna had no idea.

Without opening his eyes, he said, "My wife and daughter were killed by a drunk driver."

Sienna's lungs froze. "I'm so sorry."

"That's why I got a little too rough with the driver. I know firsthand the effects—the aftermath—of these people's actions."

"How long has it been?" She could hardly breathe as she imagined his loss.

"Three years. They were killed on impact and didn't suffer. That news did bring me some comfort."

"And your daughter? How old was she?"

"Eighteen months."

"Devin... I'm sorry."

He raised his hand. "Don't feel sorry for me. That's not why I told you. In fact, I don't really know why I told you, except that you've entrusted me with your life. I figured maybe you deserved to know some of what happened."

She searched for the right words of comfort, words that wouldn't emasculate him or make him feel pitied.

She came up with nothing.

So why did she still feel the need to speak. "Devin, I—"

Before she could finish the sentence, Devin's phone rang. He put it to his ear, and his face went a little paler. He hung up a moment later and turned to her.

"That was Detective Jenson," he started. "The police found a body in the woods not too far from Woodard's Mill."

"Okay..." Where was he going with this? Was it someone she knew?

"They believe it's Anita."

NINE

Devin watched Sienna's expression as it changed from surprise to grief.

"Anita? Are they sure?" She grabbed Devin's arm, as if needing something to steady her.

A protective surge rushed through him at her touch. "No, the police aren't sure. But she matches the basic description of the victim, and her car was found on the street nearby."

Sienna released his arm and covered her mouth with her hand. Her eyes filled with sorrow. "Did the detective say anything else? How did she die?"

"She had multiple gunshot wounds, and her body was burned beyond recognition."

Even more color left Sienna's face. She turned away from him, as if needing a moment of privacy to process everything. "That's terrible. Anita had been in danger this whole time. Maybe that's why she left Colby with me. Because she needed him to be safe."

"It's a possibility."

She swung around, her eyes wide with a new question. "What will happen to Colby now?"

"We're not sure. We're going to watch him until the police have more answers."

Fear continued to swirl in the depths of her eyes—fear over the boy's future, for his well-being, for…justice. "Did they say that I could keep watching him?"

"Not directly. But I'll make sure it happens that way. Colby doesn't need to be taken away from one of the only other people he knows right now—especially not until we have some answers."

Sienna shook her head as she turned back to the pot of boiling pasta. "This is just so terrible. What if her ex found her and demanded to know where Colby was? What if he killed her when she wouldn't say his location? Or if she did say and he killed her so she wouldn't help Colby? I don't know. I know I'm rambling and not making sense—"

"You're fine, Sienna."

She seemed to startle as she looked up at him. "Thanks for not belittling me for my talk."

Devin figured there was more to her sentence, but he didn't ask. If Sienna wanted to share, she would. "The important thing is that Colby is safe now. They won't have a positive ID on the body for a while, especially since they have nothing to identify Anita with."

"Still no hits on that?"

"No hits. Apparently, Jenson contacted the authorities in Kansas—that's where you said she went, right?"

Sienna nodded.

Devin flipped the steaks as they sizzled on the griddle. "They couldn't find anyone with her last name there who knew Anita or recognized her. They looked at the area hospitals, as well, but couldn't find anyone who matched the description of Anita or her mother. There are so many unknowns right now."

"It just doesn't make sense," Sienna muttered.

"It doesn't, does it? But it fits our theory that Anita is on the run. However, if she was on the run, why leave Colby with you?" Devin pulled the steaks off, putting them on a plate to rest for a moment.

"In case her ex—we'll just say that's who it is, but I suppose it could be any kind of enemy— found Anita, then he'd find Colby also. Maybe she figured he was safer with me."

"Something just doesn't sound right with that theory, though."

Sienna shoved her hip against the countertop and turned the burner off. "What do you mean?"

"I just mean that if I were in Anita's shoes and I was running from someone who was trying to take my child, the last thing I'd do was leave my baby with someone else. Other people might protect my child, but no one would love him or her like a parent, you know?"

Sienna nodded. "Yeah, that does make sense. But maybe there's more—more that we don't know or that we haven't guessed yet. And I suppose it doesn't matter right now. Not if Anita is dead."

"There's still a lot up in the air."

"What do we do now, Devin?" Sienna's round eyes met his.

At the emotion in her voice, Devin's heart twisted. She'd been thrown in this situation, and she'd handled it like a trouper. But there was a hint of wistfulness to her voice now.

"Now we wait. Sometimes, that's the hardest part. But it's necessary."

"And you think we're safe?"

"For now." He raised the plate of steaks. "We should eat."

Just as he said the words, Colby let out a cry from the bedroom.

The boy was awake. And that was a good thing, because if Devin stood there with Sienna any longer, looking into those big eyes of hers, he might confess that he had a really bad feeling in his gut about all of this.

With a full belly and a content Colby playing on the couch beside her, Sienna leaned back into the stiff cushions, lost in thought.

It was so much to comprehend. Anita, dead? Sienna just couldn't believe it. Her heart clutched with grief when she thought about Colby losing his mom. Who would he stay with after this storm passed? Anita's family? Did Anita even have a family capable of taking care of him? Her mother had just had hip surgery. Or would officials try to put him in foster care?

Sienna didn't know, and part of her hardly wanted to think about it. It seemed too tragic.

But it was like Devin said. Maybe the body they'd found hadn't been Anita's. Maybe the two women just shared similarities.

She just had to trust that the police were doing their jobs.

But what had Anita meant when she'd said not to trust the police? Was someone from inside the department trying to botch this? Did he or she have their own agenda?

Sienna had no idea, and her head hurt just thinking about it.

Devin sat on the other side of the couch. He stared at a yellow legal pad where he'd been scribbling notes.

Sienna found a surprising comfort in his presence. Apparently, Colby did also. He'd warmed right up to Devin, and the boy took turns sharing his toys with both Sienna and Devin. Right now, Colby played with some plastic cups Sienna had given him to stack. Instead of stacking them, he clanged them together like a percussion instrument.

"You know Anita from school, right?" Devin asked, looking up from his notepad.

"That's right. She's the teacher assistant from next door."

"Walk me through the details again. When was the last time you saw her?"

"A week ago when she dropped off Colby at my place so she could get packed up and ready to leave for her mom's hip replacement surgery." Everything had seemed so normal then, and Sienna's biggest worry had been trying to balance school work with watching Colby.

Devin leaned forward in his deep thinker pose. "How did she seem in the days before she left?"

Sienna shrugged, searching her memories for anything significant. "Normal, I guess. I mean, maybe a little stressed. I think she was nervous about her mom's surgery. Surgery can be nerve-racking, though, you know? I didn't think much of it."

He cast her a side glance before picking up a plastic cup Colby had dropped and giving it back to him. "Did anything else unusual happen during that time? Maybe at school? Or did Anita bring up anything strange in conversation?"

Again, Sienna searched back through her memories for something that might help them now. Only one thing made her pause, but she wasn't sure it was significant.

"There was this newspaper reporter who came out to the school," Sienna said. "The school administration approved it, of course. She interviewed me and a couple other teachers about a new initiative we tried this year to help the kids with reading. We solicited area restaurants and businesses to donate prizes to our top readers."

A glimmer of admiration flashed in his gaze. "What was so unusual about that?"

"Maybe nothing. But I remember that Anita walked into the room while I was being interviewed. She stopped in her tracks and went pale."

"When she saw the reporter?" Devin clarified, a knot forming between his eyebrows.

"Yes, when she saw the reporter. She excused herself and left the room, apologizing for interrupting. But when she was gone, the reporter asked a couple of questions about her. Said Anita looked familiar and asked where she was from. The reporter played it off like maybe their paths had crossed at some point."

"Did you ever ask Anita about it?"

"I was going to do. But the next day was when she asked me to watch Colby. It all seemed very sudden, which I thought was strange. Usually these surgeries are scheduled weeks in advance." Sienna shrugged and let out a long breath. "I guess I didn't think about it again until now. I figured it wasn't relevant. Some people just become really shy around the media, you know."

"Did the article ever come out?"

Sienna twisted her head in thought. "You know, now that you mention it, I don't think it has. I've been a little distracted lately, I suppose. You think it's significant?"

"Maybe that reporter did recognize Anita and that's why she acted cagey. It can't hurt to look into it."

"I agree."

"Do you have the reporter's name?"

"I have her name and cell." Sienna grabbed her purse from the floor and fished out the woman's business card. "Here it is."

Devin studied it a moment. "Lisa Daniel. But there's no newspaper on here."

"She said she freelanced for several publications. I looked her up before talking to her, and I found her byline in several places. She seemed legit. Plus, the school vetted her."

"Good to know." Devin stood.

"Are you going to call her now?"

"There's no time like the present. That's what I always say."

But before he could do anything, Sienna heard a rumble in the driveway. Her gaze veered toward Devin, but he was already on alert.

He drew his gun and rushed toward the door.
Someone was here.
The question was: Who?

TEN

"Stay down," Devin ordered softly.

He watched as Sienna took Colby and disappeared into a back bedroom. With his gun drawn, he hovered near the window and peered out.

A truck pulled up.

Whoever was driving wasn't trying to be subtle. That could be good or bad news.

Devin would reserve his judgment.

A man hopped out of the truck and sauntered toward the door. Devin observed him. The man was probably in his sixties with a long, salt-and-pepper beard and a nearly bald head. He was dressed in well-worn jeans, an old white T-shirt and a dirty khaki jacket.

He reminded Devin of a typical mountain man—someone who enjoyed the outdoors and hunting and living off the land.

He was nearly certain the man who'd broken into Sienna's house hadn't had a beard like this. It would be hard to keep it tucked into a ski mask. But he still had to be on guard.

Devin tensed as he waited to see how this would play out. A moment later, there was a knock.

He considered not answering, but his SUV was obviously parked here. Devin didn't see any weapons or anything thing else on the man outside that caused him to pause.

After lifting a quick prayer, he opened the door, concealing his gun behind the wall.

"Can I help you?" Devin asked, trying to ease the tension from his voice in order to not raise suspicions.

"Howdy," the man said. "I always come up here to check on the cabin for Jim. Saw your SUV here."

"Jim is a friend, and he said we could stay here," Devin said. "Sorry for the confusion."

"Yeah, he said someone would be here. I thought about calling him to give him the warning to give you. Then I thought it was too complicated. Besides, Jim's going through chemo right now, and I didn't want to bother him again."

"We're all praying for his health," Devin said. "What did you need to tell him?"

"Lots of people in the area have been spotting bears around here lately," he said. "And they're not shy. Wilma a few houses down the mountain was chased into her house by one. They're all over this area. Ever since they put that new neighborhood in about twenty miles from here, it's like nature has gone crazy."

"I appreciate the warning. We'll keep our eyes open."

"I know a lot of people who come out here like to hike. I just thought you should be aware. I don't want anything to happen to one of Jim's friends. A friend of his is a friend of mine."

"We will be. Thanks again." Devin watched the man walk away before closing the door.

So one more person knew they were here. It wasn't ideal, but Devin still thought they had some time to rest before they'd need to move on.

As soon as the man pulled away, he motioned that Sienna could come out.

"Is everything okay?" Sienna held Colby close, obviously protective of the boy.

"I think so. He was just trying to be a good neighbor. But the fewer people who know where we are, the better."

"I agree." She shivered and glanced around. "What now?"

"Now I'm going to try and call this reporter again." Still standing near the window—just in case someone else pulled up—Devin pulled out his phone and dialed.

Colby began fussing, so Sienna disappeared into a back bedroom with him. He was grateful for the quiet.

Devin listened to the phone ring and ring with no answer. The call went to voice mail.

What kind of reporter didn't answer her phone?

Devin would give her the benefit of the doubt. Maybe she was doing an interview and couldn't answer right now. Most reporters he'd dealt with were so curious, they couldn't pass up not knowing who was on the other end of an unknown phone number.

He left a message and hoped Lisa would call back.

In the meantime, Devin used the search engine on his phone to look for any mentions of the article Sienna was interviewed for. There was none.

It probably wasn't anything, he realized. But maybe—just maybe—this woman knew something about Anita. Maybe Lisa Daniel had some of the answers they'd been looking for.

"Devin, look at this." Sienna called him over to the computer in the spare bedroom. While Colby played with some pots and pans on the floor beside her, she'd booted up the old desktop—after asking Devin's permission, of course.

She'd done an online search for Lisa Daniel, and she'd finally hit the jackpot—she thought.

She'd found a social media site for Lisa Daniel. One of Lisa's friends, a man named Jared Anderson, had left a couple messages on her page over the past two days. Both had asked where she was and asked her to call him. He'd even left his phone number. There was no response from Lisa.

Unrest rumbled in Sienna's stomach.

Devin grunted behind her. "I'll call him."

She stood, hovering close as he dialed the number a few minutes later. She desperately wanted to hear what Jared had to say.

When she heard someone answer, she hoped they'd hit pay dirt. She leaned closer, thankful she could hear fairly well.

"Jared, this FBI Agent Devin Matthews. I'm trying to get in touch with your friend Lisa Daniel, and I wondered if you knew how I could do that."

"I've been trying to get in touch with her also," Jared said. "Is everything okay? What's this in regard to?"

Sienna could hear the worry in his voice, which was stretched tight with tension.

"This is in relation to a case we're working on," Devin said. "We need to talk to Lisa. No idea where she is?"

"No, I've been trying to call her. It's not like her not to answer."

"Have you been by her house, by chance?"

"I have. She didn't answer the door. I'm trying not to worry, but…"

"Do you know of any reason why she might

not be answering? Was there anything going on in her life that might have caused this?"

"I don't know. She was working on some article that had her all excited. Said it might be the big break she was looking for."

Devin glanced at Sienna and sent her a knowing look. "But she didn't hint what this article was about?"

"No, she said she couldn't talk about it yet," Jared said. "She had to find some more details first, but she said it was going to be a life-changing piece of journalism."

"If you hear anything, could you give me a call?" Devin asked.

"Yeah, man. Sure. I hope she's okay. I'm concerned, to say the least. She's one determined lady, and once she gets something in her head... well, there's no stopping her."

Devin ended the call and turned back to Sienna. "What do you think?"

"I think I want to talk to Lisa now more than ever." Maybe this was the clue they'd been looking for.

"Me, too." Devin clamped down, and Sienna could tell he was thinking about something.

They both glanced at Colby. He was the determining factor here. They couldn't risk exposing him—not if they didn't have to. Yet they might not be safe staying put, either.

"I have an idea to run past you," Devin said. "Let me know what you think."

An hour later, they'd left the little cabin where they'd stayed for only several hours. Soon after, Devin pulled up to a ten-foot gate with a guard station.

A man there checked his ID before returning to the guard station. He picked up a phone there, spoke to someone and then returned.

"You're cleared," the man said. "Go straight through and then veer to the right. You'll see a house on the left at the end of the road. Someone will be waiting for you there."

Devin thanked the man, raised his window back up and then pulled through the gates as they slowly opened, welcoming him inside.

"Devin, where are we?" Sienna asked, glancing around in amazement at her surroundings.

"The Jennings Center," he said. "My friend used to be special forces in the military. After he got out, he opened this place. They do special assignments for the government. Everything is hush-hush. But he and his wife live here at the headquarters. As you can see, it's almost impossible to get into this place—almost as hard as Fort Knox."

"This is fascinating. I never even knew it was here."

"People aren't supposed to know it's here.

That's the beauty of it. I'm kind of surprised I didn't think about coming here sooner. Colby will be safe here. There are multiple layers of protection to ensure that."

He followed the guard's directions and finally came to a stop at a huge log cabin—mansion was more like it—at the end of the lane. His friend Rick stepped out from the front door, a wide grin on his face as he approached Devin's door.

"It's been a long time, my friend," Rick said, a friendly smile on his face as he clamped down on Devin's shoulder. "Of course you can stay here for a while. Why don't you hop on out? I'll have one of my guys park your car for you."

He stepped out and grabbed the bag in the back. None of them had brought much. Then again, neither of them had thought this would last longer than a day. At the rate they were going, Devin had no idea when this would be over.

Rick ushered them inside, where his lovely wife, Trina, greeted them with a wide smile and a warm hug. She had a baby girl on her hip—Sarah, who was about the same age as Colby.

"I'd say you look great," Trina said teasingly.

Devin ran a hand over his scruffy chin. "Yeah, I know. It's been quite the ride over the past couple of days."

Her gaze turned to Sienna, and Devin introduced her to his friends. A spread of sandwiches and fruit salad had been laid out, and as they caught up, he, Sienna and Colby dug in.

The conversation remained lighthearted—it was like a balm to his battered emotions. Devin shouldn't have pulled away after Grace died. His friends had always been there for him, and he was wrong to put up his walls.

As they talked, Devin's phone buzzed. It was Detective Jenson.

He excused himself to answer. "What's going on?"

"We're still trying to ID the victim we found in the woods near Anita's car. The only identifying thing we could find on her was a necklace."

Devin's heart thumped in his chest. "What kind of necklace?"

"It was a crown. Can you ask Sienna if that's familiar?"

"Of course. I'll let you know."

"Thanks. And be safe. This case is giving me nightmares. I can only imagine what it's doing to you."

It was giving Devin nightmares also.

ELEVEN

As soon as Devin joined them, Sienna could see the distress on his face. But she didn't want to ask in front of everyone what that phone call had been about. He would tell her in good time.

Instead, her gaze traveled to Colby. He was grinning as he played patty cake with Sarah, Rick and Trina's daughter. The sight made her smile.

It was so good to see him having fun. Looking normal. Everything had been so crazy that this sweet moment of normalcy meant more than anything.

"Let me go show you my latest project," Rick said, motioning for Devin to follow him toward the back of the house.

"*Project* is the wrong word," Trina called. "It's a toy. A motorcycle."

"It's a beauty, that's what it is," Rick said with a grin.

As soon as they were gone, Trina turned at Sienna. "Would you like some coffee?"

"I'd love some."

She went and poured her a cup—this time with cream and sugar. As Colby and Sarah played, the two women sat at a table in front of the window overlooking the beautiful mountains.

"So, how long have you known Devin?" Trina asked.

Sienna shrugged. "Believe it or not, we've been neighbors for several months, but until several days ago, we hadn't really had a conversation."

Trina's smile faded. "I'm sorry to hear that. Devin…well, he hasn't been the same since his wife and daughter died. It was really hard on him."

"I can only imagine."

"Devin has always been the responsible type. Don't get me wrong. But he used to be able to kick back with the best of us. I hate seeing what this has done to him."

"I know it's hard to watch the people we care about suffer. Did you know his wife and daughter?"

Trina nodded, her eyes suddenly misty. "I did. They were great. The perfect family. I guess you never know when things can change and turn your world upside down."

"No, you really don't, do you?" Sienna's world had been turned upside down in a different way, she supposed, when Jackson left her, and now during this ordeal.

"Listen to me." Trina waved her hand in the air. "I'm sure you don't want to talk about all of this. You're probably exhausted. Can I get you another drink?"

"Actually, could I just use your phone? I really need to call my best friend before she gets too worried about me."

"Of course." She pulled a cell phone out of her pocket. "Why don't you let me watch Colby for a moment? You could probably use a break."

"I would really appreciate that. Thank you." Sienna disappeared back into the bedroom where she'd be staying and sank into the soft bed.

For a moment, everything felt normal. She knew this feeling wouldn't last for long, but she would enjoy it while she could. After taking in a deep breath—and inhaling the scent of lilacs and vanilla—she dialed her best friend's number.

Viviana answered on the first ring.

"It's me. Sienna."

"I didn't recognize the number and almost didn't answer," Viviana said. "I'm so glad I did."

"I'm glad you did, too. I really need to talk to you."

"I've been crazy worried. It's not like you just

to take off like this. I tried to stop by your house, and I saw the crime scene tape, and then the neighbors across the street came over and told me there was a break-in and that someone tried to take Colby. What is going on? Are you okay?"

"I'm fine. I just had to get away with Colby until we figure out what's going on."

"We?"

"I'm with… Devin."

"Your neighbor? The handsome, brooding one who looks great when he cuts the grass?"

"He's only brooding until you get to know him." Had Sienna just defended him? The realization surprised her more than anyone.

"So you've gotten to know him?" Viviana's voice held a tease.

"We've had no choice but do that. Besides, he's not ready to date. He's still mourning the loss of his wife and child."

"Oh," Viviana's voice dipped. "How long has it been?"

"Three years."

"Well, I'm sorry to hear that. Now, where are you?"

"I can't say," Sienna said, glancing around the cozy bedroom. "It's better if no one knows. But we're safe. For now."

"Who tried to take Colby?"

"That's what we're trying to figure out."

"And Anita? What's going on with her?"

Sienna remembered the news that she might be dead. "That's also a big mystery. As you know, she was supposed to be out of town helping her mother recover from hip replacement surgery."

"Yeah, I remember that."

"No one can find her."

"Sienna, I don't know if this means anything. But naturally you were the talk of the school today. Lots of rumors are going around about what's happening."

Sienna had figured as much. It was a small-town atmosphere in their little district.

"Anyway, Ms. Morris from second grade came down to my classroom, and she said the strangest thing."

"What's that?"

"She told me that she was nearly certain Anita had said at one time that both of her parents were dead."

Sienna straightened on the comfy bed, trying to process that. "That can't be right."

"That's what Ms. Morris said. She said she remembered because she also lost both of her parents. Anita told her she understood just how hard that was."

Sienna processed those words. Had Anita been lying to her this whole time? But why?

She didn't know. But she didn't like this.

* * *

When Devin came back with Rick, he glanced around, curious as to where Sienna had gone. He saw Colby happily playing with Sarah and smiled.

Coming here had been a good idea, and he couldn't think of two better people to help them than Rick and Trina.

"She went back to her bedroom to make a phone call," Trina explained.

His guard went up. "A phone call?"

Trina shrugged. "I didn't ask. I figured she was trustworthy."

"She is…"

"She seems really nice, Devin."

His felt his throat tightened. What was Trina implying? "Sienna is very nice."

"It's good seeing you with someone else. You've been alone for so long. In more ways than one."

"I appreciate what you're trying to say, Trina, but we're just friends. I don't even know if that's the right word. We're acquaintances? Neighbors? Two people thrown together in an impossible situation?"

"I didn't say you weren't. I'm just saying that this is the first time I've seen the old Devin in a long time. It's good to have you back."

He nodded, unsure what to say. But now that Trina mentioned it, he had felt more like himself over the past few days. Was it because of the case? Or was it because of Sienna and Colby? Could he possibly make room in his life for someone else one day? He doubted it.

"Grace would want you to be happy," Trina said.

Trina would know. She and Grace had been best friends. The two had met at church, and they'd been inseparable. Trina was the one Grace had shared all her secrets with. They'd shared their dreams and fears, just like two best friends were supposed to do.

That all seemed like a different lifetime sometimes—those days when the four of them had been a formidable team, in life and at the bowling alley.

For fun, they'd joined a league. Devin had never laughed as hard as he did at those competitions.

"I know Grace would want me to be happy," Devin said.

"If she saw the way you'd isolated yourself…become a shell of who you used to be… she wouldn't approve." Trina's face looked tight with concern.

"You don't think?" Devin knew the answer, he just didn't want to acknowledge it.

Trina shook her head. "No, I don't *think*. I *know* she wouldn't. Life took a terrible turn for you, Devin. A terrible turn for all of us. It's also made us realize just how little time we have here on this earth. We've got to make the best of the moments we do have. So grieve. Get it out of your system. And, in a way, you'll always have a hole where Grace and Willow used to be. But then look toward the future and try to make your way again."

Just as she said that, Sienna stepped out of the hallway.

Devin studied her face a moment, wondering if she'd overheard. Based on her expression, she hadn't seemed to.

She handed the phone back to Trina. "Thanks so much."

"You made a call?" Devin asked, trying to ignore the lump in his throat after his conversation with Trina. He would think about that later.

"Don't worry. I didn't say anything I wasn't supposed to. But I did hear something interesting."

"So did I," Devin said. "Can I grab a few minutes alone with you?"

"Of course."

"You two go. Colby is having the time of his life," Trina said.

He took her elbow and led her to the back deck. As he looked up, thousands of stars shone above them. The sight was breathtaking. Grace would have loved this. He remembered Trina's words. But Grace would have also wanted him to move on.

Sienna shared with him about what Viviana had overheard at the school about Anita's parents. He absorbed those details, not entirely surprised.

Anita had a lot of secrets. Had she taken them to the grave?

"What did you have to say?" Sienna asked, turning toward him with the starlight glinting in her hair.

She looked so beautiful that, for a moment, he forgot his words.

He hadn't felt attraction like this for so long, and he didn't know what to do with it.

Maybe Trina was right, and he needed to be more open-minded.

He'd just never expected to find these feelings in this midst of this storm, nor to find them so suddenly, so quickly.

"Jenson called," he started, clearing his throat. "They found a piece of jewelry on the body that was found burned in the woods."

Sienna sucked in a breath. "A necklace with a crown on it?"

He nodded grimly. "Yes."

She lowered her head. "It was Anita. Anita is dead."

"She had a necklace like that?"

"Yes, she wore it all the time."

"I'll let Jenson know."

Sienna let out a breath, her shoulders seeming to deflate at the action. "What are we going to do, Devin?"

"We'll figure it out." He reached over and squeezed her knee, desperate to offer some kind of comfort to the woman. "We'll find more answers tomorrow, hopefully, when we go to visit Lisa Daniel."

She raised her head. "We're going to be able to do that?"

He nodded. "I checked with Rick and Trina. They said they'd keep Colby for us. It's the only way. We can't risk taking him with us."

Sienna nodded. "You're right. We can't."

They sat there for several more minutes in silence. Devin knew he should move his hand off her knee. But he didn't. And Sienna didn't seem to mind.

"Devin? You know that message that I sent Anita via Facebook a couple of days ago?"

"Yes."

"Could I check it and see if there's any response?"

"I doubt there will be, everything considering. But, yes, you can." He pulled out his phone and handed it to her.

She typed several things in and paused, her eyes scanning something there.

"Is there a response?" he asked.

She gasped and closed her eyes before showing him the phone.

There was a message there. He wasn't sure if it was from Anita or someone else. But it read:

More people will die until Colby is mine, and their blood will be on your hands.

TWELVE

The next morning, after breakfast, Sienna said goodbye to Colby and thank you to Rick and Trina, and she took off with Devin to find out more information on Lisa Daniel. It had been wonderful to get a full night's rest without the worry of danger lingering too close for comfort. The warm meals, clean laundry and good company had also been a nice change of pace.

But last night's warning remained in her head. More people were going to die. And they were going to die because Sienna wouldn't give up Colby to the predator who was after him.

Her feelings were so mixed. She did feel guilty that other people were getting hurt. She never wanted to see that. Yet she knew she was doing the right thing. She couldn't let an innocent child be taken.

She only prayed Colby would be safe until they returned. Based on everything Sienna had seen at the Jennings Center, he would be. It would be extremely difficult for anyone to get past the security they had there.

"Are you okay?" Devin reached over and squeezed her arm, a look of concern in his eyes as he headed down the road.

Sienna nodded but the tension between her choices was tearing her apart inside.

"I guess," she finally said. "I just feel so guilty."

"That's the safest place Colby can be," Devin said. "I'm only sorry I didn't think about it earlier."

Please, Lord, help this to be the right choice.

Devin glanced at his GPS. "According to the map, we're only about forty-five minutes away from Lisa's place."

She glanced behind her. "Have you seen anyone following us?"

"Not a soul. I think we're in the clear."

"That would be amazing." Sienna stared out the window at the wooded landscape all around her. It was breathtakingly beautiful. If only she could enjoy it instead of being immersed in this tornado of trouble. "No update on the body that was found?"

"No, no update. Like I said, it's going to be difficult to ID the victim. The body was burned so badly that there are no fingerprints."

"There's got to be a way to find some answers." The police cracked cases like this all the time…didn't they? There had to be a way.

"It wouldn't surprise me if the police put out a press release on her, hoping someone can identify her," Devin said. "The tricky part is that, if Anita is alive and if she's in danger, we don't want to draw attention to her. The balance is difficult."

"I guess the police will make that call."

"They will." Devin took another sip of his coffee. Rick and Trina had let them borrow their travel mugs. Sometimes it was the small things in life that he appreciated the most. "And we have to trust them on it."

She glanced back out the window again, noting how the sun was climbing higher and higher. "Anita said don't trust the police."

"I know. There's still so much we don't know. Let's follow this lead with Lisa and see what we can find out. It might not be anything. Or it could be everything."

Sienna gripped her own coffee mug, her thoughts heavy. "I can't imagine what Lisa could have found out concerning Anita. Especially since her friend Jared said it could be a life-changing piece of journalism."

"What do you mean?"

"I mean, at first, I assumed maybe she recognized Anita, and Anita didn't want to be recognized because she's running from her ex. But that doesn't fit with the life-changing part. I mean, it would change Anita's life, for sure. But journalism is generally a bigger story than that, you know?"

"I agree," Devin said. "Maybe there's more to this story, and we're just scratching the surface here."

"Maybe we are." Sienna leaned back, trying to gain control of her thoughts before they turned into full-fledged anxiety.

"I think you're doing great here, Sienna." Devin cast a kind smile at her.

Hearing the sincerity in his voice brought a flush of warmth across her skin. He'd been kind to her yesterday as well when she'd started rambling. Jackson could never stand that about her. If she rambled, it drove him crazy until he finally blew a gasket. He'd become a different person once they started dating, but she'd assumed it was the stress of starting a new job and a new life.

She knew it had to be a lot of pressure for him with all the big life changes that were taking place all at once. But she'd been going through a lot of life changes herself, and she hadn't acted like a jerk as a result.

Looking back, it was a blessing that he'd called

off the wedding. It had just taken her a while to see it.

"Thanks," Sienna finally said. "I feel like a mess."

"I can't tell by looking at you."

"I just want what's best for Colby, you know?"

"Yeah, I do." The wistfulness in his voice caused a pang to rush through her.

Was Devin thinking of his own daughter? His wife? Sienna couldn't even imagine what he'd been through or how hard losing both a wife and child would be. It explained why he'd acted so distant. The man was grieving after his life had been upended.

"Here's Lisa's place." Devin pulled up to a small cottage nestled in an older neighborhood on the outskirts of Denver. "You ready for this?"

"I'm ready. Let's do this."

Devin pounded on the door to Lisa's home and waited.

He hoped—for Colby and Sienna's sakes—they'd find some answers.

But since Lisa wasn't answering her phone and her friend hadn't seen her in two days, he was anxious to see if she'd be here.

Just as he expected, there was nothing.

"What now?" Sienna turned toward him, her lips pulling down in a frown.

He glanced around, looking for any neighbors

who might be peering out their windows, looking nosy. Sometimes they could be the best sources of information.

He didn't have to look too hard, because a car pulled up just then and a man hopped out, waddling their way with urgency in his steps.

The man was short and pudgy, and a huge set of keys dangled at his belt. His outfit—a dirty blue button-up shirt and matching slacks—gave the impression that he was a handyman or janitor.

"You looking for Lisa?" the man asked, rushing past them toward the door.

The name tag on his shirt read "Frank."

"We are," Devin said. "Have you seen her?"

The man paused and looked at both Devin and Sienna over. "I work with a company that manages this rental. I've been looking for her also. I have someone coming in to work on her AC, and she won't answer my texts."

"How long have you been trying to contact her?" Devin asked.

"Two days. And no answer. I can't believe it. She was the one who was so concerned about this AC and the fact that it was going to start getting hotter and hotter outside."

The two days fit the time frame they'd already established.

Devin reached into his pocket and pulled out

his badge. "I'm FBI. I need to get into the house concerning an investigation."

Frank turned from annoyed to worried. "Of course. Is everything okay?"

"We hope so," Devin said. "We just want to confirm that."

"Then so be it." Frank looked through his inventory of keys, unlocked the door and shoved it open. "Be my guest."

Devin motioned for Sienna to wait outside while he checked out the interior. With his gun in hand, he made his way into the living room and surveyed the simple but well-decorated space. It seemed to fit the image of Lisa Daniel he had in his mind.

The house was clear.

So far.

Devin continued past the living room and into the kitchen and dining room.

Nothing gave any indication that a struggle had happened here. Everything was in place and neat, almost like the woman had been planning a photo shoot later. He wondered if Lisa always kept her place this way. He'd have to ask Frank, just in case it was important.

As Devin started down the hall toward the bedrooms, he saw movement. He raised his gun just as a figure darted from the hallway.

His heart rate surged.

Someone was in the house. Someone dressed in all black and with a ski mask.

The intruder pushed past him, throwing Devin temporarily off balance.

As Devin straightened, the man was already at the door. If Devin took a shot now, he might hit Sienna or Frank.

He couldn't risk that.

Instead, Devin took off after the man, determined to catch him and finally get some answers.

He stepped out just in time to see the intruder brush past Sienna. She flew back into the door frame, her eyes widening in alarm.

Devin continued forward, pausing for just long enough to ask Sienna, "Are you okay?"

She looked shaken but she nodded. "Yes. Don't worry about me. Go get him."

Devin's leg muscles burned as he pushed himself across the lawn. The man had already hit the street.

He'd had a head start. Maybe too much of a head start.

But Devin was fast. He knew that. Maybe he could catch him.

That man had been in Lisa's house for a reason. Devin needed to figure out what that reason was. The easiest way? It would be by catching this guy and asking him face-to-face. He was tired of all of these guessing games.

Devin's muscles continued to strain as he rushed across the grass to the sidewalk. The man reached the other side of the street and kept going.

Devin's foot hit the asphalt, about to cross the road. As he did, a car appeared out of nowhere, headed right toward him. The bumper hit the side of Devin's thigh as the vehicle screeched to a stop.

Devin ignored the pain pulsing through him and skirted around the car. He couldn't afford to take his eyes off the intruder, and he couldn't let an injury slow him up. He would deal with that later.

Who was this guy? Devin quickly studied him as he pushed himself forward. The man was dressed in all black from head to toe. He appeared to be fairly fit. On the taller side.

It was clear the man was desperate. Totally desperate as he ran away, his motions scattered and frantic.

Just as the man reached the next block, a maroon-colored car squealed to a stop at the curb. The man opened the door and jumped inside. Before Devin could reach them, the car accelerated away.

Devin stopped there on the corner and sucked in several deep breaths as he watched the car disappear. He would have gotten the plate numbers, but the plates were gone.

But a woman sat in the driver's seat.

Had that been Lisa? Or Anita? Or was it some-one totally different?

He had no idea. But right now, he needed to check on Sienna and try to figure out what that man was trying to retrieve from the house.

THIRTEEN

Sienna pulled her arms across her chest as her heart raced out of control.

What was going on? Where was Devin? Was he okay?

She hardly knew the man, yet she felt like she did. The connection she felt with Devin…it was strange. Surprising. Exciting.

With every new turn in the road and clue that was revealed, Sienna found a new respect for the man.

"I don't know what's going on here, but it's like crazy town," the landlord said, still staring at the chase in bewilderment.

She tried to tune him out. All she cared about was knowing Devin was okay. That he hadn't gotten hurt or even killed because of this crazy situation.

No one else needed to get hurt. No, there was too much of that already.

Finally, she spotted Devin walking back toward them. Based on the stoop of his shoulders, he wasn't happy. He was also empty-handed.

What had happened out there? Her heart pitter-pattered with both anticipation and disappointment.

She'd so hoped he would catch this man and put an end to all their questions. But, as it had been from the start, whoever was responsible for these crimes was two steps ahead of them.

Sienna walked down the steps and met Devin on the lawn. Instinctively, she reached for him, grabbing his arm, needing to touch him and know he really was fine. He had a slight limp to his step, and she'd seen the car hit him. The driver had stayed around for several minutes, looking flabbergasted about what to do. Finally, he'd driven off.

"Are you okay?" Sienna asked, her voice thin with emotion.

Devin nodded, but he didn't look okay, and he definitely didn't act happy. "He got away."

Sienna had figured that much. "Any idea who he was?"

"No idea. But he wanted something in that house."

"How do you know he didn't get it?" Was there hope that whatever the sought-after object was, that it could still be inside?

Devin rubbed his leg, his eyes squeezing together in discomfort. "I don't know that. But he was empty-handed. I figure that's a good sign."

"Maybe there is a clue inside—something that will tell us what this is all about." Hope rose inside Sienna. That had to be getting close. At least they were on the right trail.

"We'll go inside and look. First, let me call the car in. Maybe a state trooper can stop it."

Just as Devin pulled his phone out, Frank ended a phone call he'd been actively engaged in on the porch and rushed down the steps. He looked aghast at everything that had happened.

"I don't want any part of this," Frank rushed, waving his hand in the air dramatically. "I don't like trouble."

"We'll be out of your hair soon," Devin said. "As soon as we check out the inside."

Devin stepped away and muttered something into the phone. As he did, Frank continued to ramble, just as he had been doing ever since the man in black had darted from the house. The problem was, he wasn't saying anything new. No, just the same things over and over.

"Lisa seemed like a good girl, you know," Frank repeated. "She was a reporter. Ambitious. You could see it in her eyes that once she got something in her mind, she wasn't going to back down. Like this AC. That's why I was surprised when she didn't answer my calls."

Sienna could remember seeing that look in Lisa's gaze. The woman was determined and likable. She seemed like the kind of person you wanted to have on your side when things went south, because she would fight for you.

Who was Lisa fighting for now?

And, even more, who was fighting for her?

Sienna's heart ached at the thought. The fact that no one had seen or heard from her in two days wasn't a good sign.

Devin put his phone away and turned to Sienna. "The police will be on the lookout for the sedan. In the meantime, let's go check things out."

After walking through the front end of the house, they ventured back toward the bedrooms—Devin told her that was where the intruder had come from. Sienna's gut told her that was where they'd find anything they were looking for.

The second room had been converted into an office and guest bedroom. Devin sat in the chair and began to go through the file drawers while Sienna riffled through the items atop the desk. She found nothing.

After several minutes, it was apparent that Devin hadn't found anything, either. He turned back to the computer atop her desk and hit a key. The screen came to life.

Just what was on there? Did the secrets about

her upcoming article hide within the interfaces and files within the electronics?

"I'm not going to be able to get on this," Devin said. "It's passcode protected. Maybe some of the guys at the bureau can."

Just then, something caught Sienna's eye—a fleck of pale yellow sticking out from behind the desk. She reached for the mystery object and slid a manila folder out. It looked like Lisa had been trying to conceal it.

"We may not have to get on the computer," Sienna said, dread pooling in her stomach.

"Why's that?"

She showed him the file that she opened. There, right on top, was a picture along with official text beneath it from the National Center for Missing and Exploited Children. "It looks like Lisa was investigating a kidnapped baby."

Devin's gaze shot up to Sienna's, and he reached for the file. "What?"

Sienna sat on the edge of the bed. "It's true. This baby was only seventeen months old when he disappeared. It's a boy named Liam Brighton."

Devin studied Sienna a moment. He could hear the grief in her voice, and he understood it. The implications of this…they were horrible. "You think that boy—Liam—is Colby?"

Sienna's gaze went to the picture, and she traced the image with her finger. "I really can't tell based on the picture. I mean, babies change so quickly every day. He has the right skin color. He's the right age."

"Does Colby have any distinguishing marks or features that might help us identify him?"

She pressed her lips together. "He has a little birthmark on his leg, on his upper thigh. It's about the size of a pea. Light brown. You wouldn't know it was there unless you've changed his diaper."

Devin studied the paper. There was no mention of a birthmark. "I could put in a call to find out. Then again, this could be a separate story."

"It could be. But what if it's not?"

"Let's keep looking through her desk, just to be sure there's nothing else. I'll call about this lead, okay?"

Sienna nodded.

He stepped into the hall to make the request for more information. Then he took a picture of the boy on his phone. He needed to find out everything he could.

Because no one was safe until they had some answers.

He didn't tell Sienna everything about the earlier chase. No, he didn't tell her that the woman driving the car very well could have been Anita.

They continued to look through things at Lisa's until Devin's phone rang again twenty minutes later. It was his contact.

And yes, indeed, the kidnapped baby—Liam Brighton—had a birthmark.

Sienna leaned back into the leather seat of Devin's SUV as they headed down the road and away from Lisa Daniel's place. "I still can't believe this. I can't believe Colby could be this kidnapped child. Then that means…"

"It means Anita may have kidnapped him," Devin finished quietly. "It's the only thing that makes sense."

"Why leave Colby with me?" The questions had been taunting Sienna ever since she'd heard the update. She'd been trying and trying to make sense of each uncertainty, but she'd had zero success.

"I have no idea what Anita might have been thinking." Devin gripped the steering wheel as they headed down the road. "Maybe she really did have to take care of her mom after surgery."

"I'd think Anita would take Colby with her then. And who was the man who tried to snatch him? Is he connected with Anita? Or someone else?" The questions poured out of her, needing some place to go. If they stayed inside her, Sienna might lose her mind.

"What if the man who's been trying to snatch Colby is his birth father? What if they tracked down Colby and think you took him?"

Sienna shrugged, considering the possibility. "I'm not ruling anything out, but it seems like a stretch. Still, people have done crazier things. This situation is a case in point."

"I agree. But I'm just trying to think of this from every possible angle."

"What are we going to do now?" Sienna turned toward him, anxious to hear his opinion on where they should go after learning this new development. They'd pulled out of town, but they hadn't gotten to the interstate yet.

Devin stole a glance at her. "I say we go pay this couple, the Brightons, a visit."

"Aren't they four hours away?" Colby's image flashed into Sienna's mind. That was a long time to be away from him. How was he doing? Did he miss her? Did he sense something was wrong?

"They are about four hours away," Devin said. "Can you handle it?"

She crossed her arms over her chest as she contemplated the question. "I do think we should talk to them. I think it's important. But what about Colby?"

"I'll call Rick and Trina and see if they can watch him longer—if you're okay with it."

Sienna twisted her lips. "He did look happy, didn't he? I mean, he loves being around other kids."

"I think he'll be fine. We can be back tonight at the earliest or tomorrow morning at the latest."

"I think I don't have a choice. We've got to get to the bottom of this. In the long run, this is what's best for Colby."

"I agree."

Sienna's eyelids drooped as the miles continued past. She was so tired. Everything felt like it was catching up with her, and this was so far from over.

"Why don't you get some rest?" Devin said, casting a concerned glance her way. "We have a long drive. I'll stop in a few hours for some food. But until then, you should try and sleep."

"I hate to make you stay awake the whole time. Are you sure I can't help you drive?"

"I'm sure. But thank you."

"Okay then." Sienna closed her eyes and leaned her head against the seat back. Maybe some rest would be the best thing. She only hoped she *could* rest with all the anxiety-inducing thoughts going through her head.

Devin kept one eye on his rearview mirror. Was that car following them? He wasn't sure.

But he knew it was a possibility that the man

who'd been in Lisa's house had waited for them to leave so he could figure out Sienna and Colby's location. Devin was doing his best to get off the interstate and take back roads as he tried to lose the other car.

He wove in and out of traffic, slowing down and speeding up to see if any cars would match his pattern. None did. Finally, he was satisfied that no one was behind him.

After being on the road for two hours, he looked for a restaurant to eat. If they stopped now, then they should arrive at the Brightons' house around five. It seemed like perfect timing.

As he pulled into the parking lot of a local diner and put the car in Park, he started to nudge Sienna but stopped himself.

She looked so peaceful as she lay there with her lips slightly apart. He almost hated to wake her.

Sienna had surprised him. The woman was selfless and kind. She was smart and caring.

Maybe Devin had known she was for a long time—and maybe that was why he'd stayed away. Maybe he'd known in his subconscious that Sienna would be too tempting.

And she was.

Devin squeezed his eyes shut.

Grace, why did you have to leave me so early? We had so much life left together. How do I navigate all of this with you gone?

Of course, there was no answer. But Devin pictured his beautiful wife's face in his mind.

And she didn't look happy.

No, she almost looked like she was ready to scold him. To tell him that it had been three years and he needed to move on. That it was okay.

No, that certainly couldn't be correct. Grace was his one love. Devin wouldn't ever find a love like that again. Not in this lifetime. They hadn't been a perfect couple, but they had seemed perfect for each other. She understood his need to be alone to reflect when times felt overwhelming. She gave him space to do his job without making him feel guilty. She loved him despite his flaws, which were many.

And Devin had loved Grace despite her flaws, as well. Even though she tended to be messy. Even though she tended to worry and wanted to talk endlessly about all the bad possibilities. Even though she insisted chocolate and peanut better was the worst combination ever.

He smiled when he thought about their discussions on the topic.

Grace had been one in a million. But she was gone, and the rest of his life stretched before him.

Devin's gaze came back into focus as Sienna began to stir.

She glanced over at him, and her cheeks flushed. She straightened and ran a hand through her hair, tousling her silky locks. "We're here. You should have woken me."

"I was just about to. I just pulled in and thought we could grab a bite to eat."

Her shoulders seemed to relax. "That sounds good. I am a little hungry."

He nodded toward Louise's Kitchen. "Great. Let's go."

FOURTEEN

Sienna and Devin slid into an old vinyl booth at the outdated, home-style restaurant that smelled like a mix of bacon and potpourri. Several people stopped to stare as soon as they'd stepped inside.

This was obviously a small town, one that was wary of visitors.

Sienna ignored them. She'd grown up in a small town, so she knew all about those dynamics.

A waitress with gray hair pulled into a sloppy bun approached them and handed them two ice waters and some laminated menus.

"Specials are on the board," she said, a smile nowhere to be seen.

It was just as well that the woman wasn't very friendly. Sienna wasn't feeling overly social, either.

She glanced at the selections on the menu, not especially hungry yet famished at the same time. She needed to eat if she was going to keep her energy up. She finally decided on a burger and fries. The waitress returned a moment later, and Sienna ordered. Devin got the pot roast with mashed potatoes.

"How's your leg?" Sienna asked Devin once she was sure there'd be no more interruptions for a while.

"It's sore." He rubbed his thigh where the vehicle had hit him.

"That SUV got you pretty hard."

"It did. But I'll just have a bruise. Nothing I won't recover from."

Sienna played with her straw wrapper, feeling surprisingly comfortable with her once-aloof neighbor. How quickly things could change.

Being in a situation like this really let you see someone's true colors. And Sienna was glad she had seen Devin's true colors, because she liked them. Her first impression of the man had been dead wrong.

"You plan on going back to work for the FBI one day?" she asked.

Devin nodded slowly. "Yeah, I do. I love my job."

"It's good to love what you do." She understood because she loved teaching—she loved her students and adored their innocent hugs and wide smiles. It reminded her of how much hope there was in life, even if it was hard to see.

Devin shifted, his gaze steady. "Now my turn for a question."

"Sure. Go ahead."

"Have you dated since you and your fiancé broke up?"

Sienna nibbled her bottom lip a moment, surprised at his question. "I have been on a grand total of three dates since then. Two were men my friends set me up with and one was a man I met in the grocery store."

"No interest?"

She shook her head. "No, no interest. I think after you're dumped like I was, you realize what you're looking for in a man."

"And what's that?"

Her cheeks heated, though she wasn't sure why. Or maybe she was. Could it be because Devin's face had flashed through her mind? "Someone who's loyal. Stable. Whose emotions don't toss him all over the place. Who respects me and my thoughts, even when they don't make sense to him."

"Your ex didn't do those things?"

"I can't say he did." She rubbed her cup of water absently, moving the beads of moisture up and down. "I've just learned to steer clear of that kind of personality type."

"I see."

"How about you? Have you dated since…"

She couldn't finish the question. And, even with only the first part leaving her lips, Sienna regretted it. Losing a spouse and daughter to death was different than being left at the altar. She'd opened up a wound that may have never completely healed.

"No, I haven't. I suppose I haven't found anyone who interests me. And…well, it's difficult to put the past behind me." His words contained a wistfulness that touched Sienna.

"I understand."

As a moment of awkwardness fell between them, the waitress appeared with their food. The plates looked delicious, and Sienna hoped the dishes tasted as good as they smelled. They joined hands for a moment of prayer before digging in.

Just as Sienna had taken the first bite, she noticed the man sitting across from them. He stared them down, an unmistakably bitter look in his eyes. She tried to ignore him and continue eating, but she couldn't.

"Devin, this could be nothing, but there's a man who looks like he wants to rip our heads off. Don't turn too quickly."

He nodded subtly, took a bite of his roast and then gazed around the restaurant.

The man nearly snarled at them as soon as Devin's head turned his way.

The next thing Sienna knew, the man was on his feet and storming toward their table.

She braced herself for whatever was about to happen.

Devin rose to his feet, quick to put himself between this man and Sienna. "Can I help you?"

"I heard about you two," the man growled, his gaze stony and accusatory.

Devin bristled, wondering where the man was going with this. "Heard about us?"

The man jutted his finger out toward Devin and Sienna. "You two are with that development company. You want to turn our mountain into a neighborhood."

Devin exchanged a glance with Sienna. She looked equally confused. Where in the world had the man gotten that idea?

"Why would you think that?" Devin asked.

The man threw his thumb behind him, his posture still looking wound up and ready for a fight. "The man in the parking lot stopped and warned me about you two. He told me who you are."

Devin's spine stiffened at his words. "Wait— the man in the parking lot? When did he tell you this?"

"A few minutes ago, before I walked in. Why? What's that matter? You trying to deflect from the issue here? Because you two aren't welcome in this town. Do I need to escort you out?"

"Hold that thought."

Without asking anymore questions, Devin darted toward the door. He knew it was a long shot, but he had to see if the man was still there. Because that man had to be the one following them. He had to be.

As soon as Devin stepped outside, he paused. Bright sunlight hit him, and two rows of cars stared back. No one was in sight—only a lone road in the distance that carried travelers to and from their destinations.

Devin examined each of the windows of the vehicles. He stopped at a truck that had signs and stickers plastered all over it, proclaiming Stop Development.

Go Away Hayman Corp.

Leave Our Mountain Alone.

That had to belong to the man inside. It would have been easy for the man pursuing Devin and Sienna to find the right motivation to enlist this guy into helping.

He scanned the rest of the vehicles. No one was inside the cars.

Whoever that man had been, he was now gone.

But the bad feeling in Devin's gut remained.

He rushed back inside and saw Sienna still sitting at the table. She talked to the mountain man, who had seemed to calm down. Knowing Sienna, she could make the gruffest of persons warm up to her. She just had that way about her.

"Did you find him?" Sienna asked, her voice nearly breathless with hope as she looked up at Devin.

Devin shook his head, wishing he had better news. "No, he was gone."

"Your girlfriend here explained to me that you're not with the developers," the man said, his demeanor notably calmer. "I apologize for the misunderstanding. It's a sensitive topic around here."

Devin didn't bother to correct his assumption about Sienna being his girlfriend. It wasn't the most important issue right now. "No, we're definitely not developers or anything close. That man was just trying to lead you astray."

The man narrowed his eyes with doubt.

Devin pulled out his badge and flashed it. "I'm FBI. Now, could you tell us what this man looked like and exactly what he said?"

"Sure. He was tall." He motioned with his hands to illustrate, showing a man around Devin's height. "Kind of big across the shoulders. Had dark hair and a look of determination in his eyes."

Devin absorbed the man's words. It fit the description of the man Devin had encountered at Lisa Daniel's place and even at Sienna's on the night all of this had begun. Devin had never seen his face, but he knew the body type, at least.

"And what exactly did he say?" Devin asked.

"Please think carefully, because it's vitally important to a case I'm working."

"I was about to come inside when he stopped me." The man rubbed his wiry beard. "He warned me that you'd be inside and told me that, if I was opposed to the development, I should let you know you're not welcome here."

"You didn't think that was unusual?" Devin asked.

"People around here are against development. This has been our mountain for generations. We'll do whatever we have to do to stop that neighborhood from going in."

So someone had obviously known that. But why had the man wanted to draw attention to Devin and Sienna? Had he wanted to slow them up so he could get a head start? Did that mean he was headed to the Brightons', as well?

The questions churned inside Devin, and suddenly his appetite was gone.

"Thank you for your help." Devin pulled out his wallet and dropped some cash on the table. "Sienna, I think we should go. Now."

Sienna was still shaken from the confrontation in the restaurant. Her mind kept replaying it as she and Devin headed down the road.

She just couldn't figure out this person's game plan, no matter how much she turned it over in her mind.

"These people know our every move, it seems," Sienna said, glancing at Devin. His profile showed that he was equally distracted by the earlier scene. He had that determined look in his eyes. His jaw kept flexing as if he were deep in thought.

"I know. But I'm certain we weren't followed. I kept my eye on the road. That's why this doesn't make sense to me."

"To me, either." She crossed her arms and leaned back, exhausted from all the running and all the questions and worry. She glanced over at Devin again, a new question rising in her mind. "You mind if I check on Colby?"

"Not at all."

He handed her his phone, and she dialed Trina's number. She answered on the first ring, sounding breathless but friendly.

"I was wondering when you'd call," Trina said.

"Is everything okay?"

"Oh, everything is fine. Colby is having a great time."

Relief filled Sienna. She'd suspected he was, but it was good to hear a confirmation. "Great. I'm so glad to hear that. Thanks again for taking care of him. It means a lot."

"It's no problem at all. Sarah is happy to have a friend to play with. And if Sarah is happy, I'm happy. We've already built a monster tower of blocks, we've made cookies and I'm toying with the idea of finger painting next. Pray for me."

Sienna smiled. Trina was the kind of friend she wanted one day when she had kids of her own—if that ever happened. Sometimes it didn't seem like it would. Being dumped by Jackson had shaken her self-confidence, she supposed.

"There is one thing." Trina's voice changed from lighthearted to serious.

Sienna's spine stiffened as she sensed bad news coming. "What's that?"

"Colby accidentally pulled his diaper bag down from the table today, and everything fell out all over the floor."

"Okay…" Sienna had no idea where she was going with this, but so far it didn't sound too serious.

"Anyway, as I was putting things back inside, I noticed the bottom of the bag liner was loose. I tried to readjust it, but the whole thing came out. There was one of those tracking tiles beneath the plastic insert there."

Sienna knew a little about the devices. They were little plastic squares that a person could connect with their phones. People usually attached them to keys or cell phones or other objects that they didn't want to lose. That way, if they did lose something, they could ping the tile, which would show them where it was located.

"What?" What sense did that make?

"I didn't think it was yours. I did a little research, and this particular brand pings off other Bluetooth tiles in the area, so it has a broader tracking range. Up to a few miles, if what I read was correct."

"So someone could track the location of the diaper bag even from far away," Sienna muttered, a sick feeling in her gut.

"Exactly. The device was wedged in so tightly that I can't imagine it got there by accident."

"Thanks for letting me know. I worry that someone might trace it to you—and Colby—there at the Jennings Center.

"I understand. I already researched how to disable it, but I didn't find a lot of great ideas. I could burn it."

"Don't do that. The police may be able to use it to track back to the person who placed it there originally. Just..." What could she do?

"There's an area here where cell service is restricted. I'll store it there. Nothing pings in that area. Believe me."

"That sounds great. Thank you."

"Of course. Anyway, I just thought you'd want to know, in case it was important."

Sienna ended the call and relayed the conversation to Devin.

His jaw visibly tightened. "Now we know how they've been following our moves. They planned from the start to keep track of us by planting that in the diaper bag."

"It also means they know where Colby is," Sienna said, her stomach twisting with disgust. Whatever was going on here, it had been planned. Intentional. Premeditated.

"But they can't get to Colby," Devin reminded her. "Remember that."

That did bring her a measure of comfort.

"It doesn't explain how they found us today," Sienna said.

"Maybe he was watching and waiting for us to leave Lisa's place," Devin said.

"But you said we weren't followed."

Devin let out a long breath. "I suppose once we got out of town and headed down this road, there weren't very many places we could go. This guy could have hung back far enough that I wouldn't spot him, continued down the road, and then seen our car here at Louise's Kitchen."

It was plausible, Sienna mused. "You think he knows we're going to the Brightons'?"

"Not necessarily. But we should be careful. Because the more I learn, the more uncomfortable I am."

Sienna pulled her arms more tightly around herself, understanding his statement all too well. "Me, too. Me, too. And I just can't reconcile in my mind why he would do this. Was he trying to slow us down? Stop us?"

"I suppose there could be a myriad of reasons. But maybe the main one is that he doesn't want us to talk to the Brightons."

"Which means that's exactly what we should do."

Devin glanced at her and nodded, admiration in his gaze. "Exactly."

FIFTEEN

Sienna paused outside the home of George and Joyce Brighton, feeling an unusual amount of nerves rushing through her limbs at the possibility of the upcoming conversation.

Lord, please guide our words. Guard this couple's heart. Give us wisdom.

The couple lived in a small house with white vinyl siding and badly neglected flower beds that had probably been beautiful at one time, based on the landscaping layout. Now they were overrun with weeds—a byproduct of trauma? Most likely.

The sun was still in the sky, but it was starting to sink lower. Another day was almost coming to an end. It was hard to believe how much had changed so quickly. How in the blink of an eye Sienna's life had been turned into a living, breathing nightmare.

There was so much at stake here, Sienna reminded herself. Not just for her and Colby, but for this couple they were about to talk to. She and Devin had to be careful not to get the Brightons' hopes up—not until they knew for sure what was going on.

"You ready for this?" Devin asked, touching her elbow lightly.

His touch sent a wave of reassurance through her. Funny how quickly she'd already begun to depend on him.

Sienna nodded, even though she didn't really know for sure. She just had to get this over with.

Devin rang the bell, and a moment later a couple in their midforties appeared. Both looked confused at their arrival, but Sienna and Devin hadn't wanted to announce themselves before coming. No, Devin said they should get a gut reaction from the couple, and she was going to have to trust him on this. Warning them seemed so much kinder.

"Can we help you?" Joyce asked.

Sienna recognized her from the photos of the couple she'd scoped out online. Joyce was tall with light brown hair that had been peppered with white strands. She had circles under her eyes that made her look older than her forty-four years.

Sienna wondered if Joyce had always looked this worn down or if grief had aged her too quickly. She'd guess it was losing her child that had done it.

"I'm Devin Matthews, special agent with the Denver office of the FBI. Could we have a minute of your time?"

"We were just sitting down to eat dinner," George said, a wary look in his eyes. "But, yes, come inside."

George also looked like his online photos. He was tall and thin with about ten pounds of extra weight in his stomach. He had long sideburns and thinning reddish-brown hair on the top of his head.

Devin and Sienna stepped into a cozy home. The inside wasn't anything fancy, but it was clean and tidy. The scent of garlic lingered in the air, and Sienna would guess the couple had been about to eat some kind of Italian meal.

Sienna sucked in a deep breath when she saw the photos on the wall beside her.

Photos of a baby. Photos of a happy Joyce and George holding the boy. In one picture they were at the park and the boy was in a baby swing. In another, the Rocky Mountains stood majestically behind all three of them. Another was taken at a studio with a gray background. They all looked so happy in each of the photos.

Sienna's heart twisted with grief. These people had been through so much.

Lord, help us not to get their hopes up, not to later dash them. So much could go wrong here.

Her stomach squeezed hard with dread.

"Would you like to have a seat?" Joyce motioned to the couch.

"I'd hate for your food to get cold," Devin said. "Are you sure you don't want to eat?"

"We can reheat it. I don't think I could right now if I wanted to." Joyce wrung her hands together, obviously nervous. "Please, have a seat."

Devin and Sienna sat beside each other on the couch, while George and Joyce sat in wing-back chairs across from them. Their expressions had an apprehensive look, as if they were nervous and their minds fought worst-case scenarios.

"What's going on? Is this about Liam? Is he…" George's voice broke.

He was afraid they were going to tell him they'd found a body, wasn't he?

Sienna's regret churned harder.

"We haven't found any bodies," Devin said, snapping into professional mode. "Let me just stop that thought right there. We don't know if this pertains to Liam at all. I'm working another case, and I had a few questions about what happened."

Joyce's hand covered her mouth. "Oh no. Please tell me another child wasn't taken."

"Ma'am, please don't become alarmed. At this point, I'm just asking questions and gathering information."

George squeezed Joyce's hand as she nodded. "Of course."

Devin pulled in a long, deep breath. Sienna could tell this was hard for him since he'd dealt with loss himself. He knew how grief worked. How it could change people.

"I've read the reports on what happened, Mr. and Mrs. Brighton," Devin said. "But I'd still like to hear for myself what happened. Would that be okay?"

"Yes, yes," Joyce said. "Where should I start?"

"Tell me about the moment you realized your son was gone." Devin's words stretched across the room.

Sienna held her breath as she waited for the couple to respond. She couldn't even imagine what they'd gone through—a parent's worst nightmare. And to still have no answers only extended that nightmare. It had to be unbearable.

The couple glanced at each other, volumes spoken between them—volumes that heartache had created and forged. The landscape of their lives had been irrevocably changed.

"I woke up in the morning and got ready for work, just like I always do," Joyce said. "Liam was a sleeper. He's always liked his naps."

Colby was a good sleeper also. Was that just a coincidence? Sienna tried to reserve her opinion, but that was proving to be difficult so far. She felt certain that Colby was their child.

"When it was time to wake him up, I went into his room. I moved his blanket, thinking he was beneath it. But, deep inside, I knew something was wrong from the moment I woke up that morning. The crib was empty." Joyce's voice broke as she covered her mouth.

"Was there any sign of forced entry?" Devin asked.

George swung his head back and forth. "No. None. And we didn't hear a thing that night."

"Who else had a key to your place?" Devin continued.

"No one," Joyce said. "We moved here three years ago without any family or anyone else in the area. I suppose we're slow to trust people."

Strange. How had someone gotten in? Had the intruder picked the lock? It seemed like a possibility. How else would you explain it?

"Do you work, Joyce?" Devin asked. "I'm just gathering information so I can put the whole picture together. I know it may seem irrelevant, but it's not."

"I do. I'm a nurse. George is an electrician. Unfortunately, we both have to work in order to pay for housing in this area."

"And where did Liam go while you were at work?"

"He went to a day care," Joyce said. "A good one—one of the best in the area, for that matter."

Devin nodded. "Are you involved with a

church or anything else where people may have seen or interacted with Liam?"

"We did just start going to a church around that time, but we weren't involved." Joyce grabbed a tissue and balled it in her hands— just in case she needed it, it appeared. "We'd only gone twice before Liam disappeared, and we kept Liam with us during the services. I liked to be with him as much as I could. In fact, it broke my heart to leave him at day care, but we had little choice."

"I can imagine," Sienna said.

"At least it was only for two days a week," Joyce continued. "I was able to adjust my work schedule, even though it meant George and I didn't see each other as much. But to answer your original question, no. There's no one at church or at the day care who could be a suspect."

"Good to know," Devin said.

"We wanted a baby so badly but couldn't have one," George explained, his face and voice tight with emotion. "We went through in vitro. It didn't work. We tried to adopt. It fell through. And then, just when we'd given up, we found out we were pregnant. It was such a blessing from God. And then it was ripped away from us."

A cry escaped from Joyce, and George put his arm around her.

Sienna glanced at Devin and saw the compassion on his face.

She'd underestimated the man. There was a lot more to him than she'd ever imagined.

Then again, tragedy was a great teacher of compassion.

"I'm sorry to you both," Devin said. "I can't imagine what you've been through."

"Do you have a lead, Agent Matthews?" George asked, his voice catching.

"I wouldn't call it a lead," Devin said. "But we're looking into another case. We came across some research from a reporter named Lisa Daniel."

Joyce's eyes lit. "Lisa? I've been trying to get in touch with her."

"So you do know her?" Devin's voice lilted with curiosity.

"She contacted us about three weeks ago," George said. "She said she wanted to do a story on Liam's kidnapping. She did an extensive interview with us about it. Last time we talked to her, she said she had a lead she wanted to explore, and she was supposed to be in touch."

"Did she say anything else?" Devin asked, hope growing in his voice.

"No, she didn't. She promised to call us with an update, but we never heard from her." Joyce stared at them with wide eyes. "Is she okay? Did something happen?"

"We don't know, but we're looking into her disappearance." Devin pulled out his phone and found a picture there. "Mr. and Mrs. Brighton, have you ever seen this woman before?"

Joyce gasped. "That's Ruth. She worked at Liam's day care. But she left a month before he disappeared. Said she had to move back home to take care of her mother, who was having surgery. Hip replacement."

All the blood seemed to leave Sienna's face until all she could hear was the pounding of her heart in her ears.

Ruth?

Was Anita not a victim of abuse at all? Was she really a kidnapper living under an assumed identity instead?

How could Sienna have been so blind?

SIXTEEN

Devin gripped the steering wheel as they left the house and made their way back toward where Colby was staying.

With every new bit of information he learned, he became more uncomfortable. This conversation with the Brightons had only solidified the bad feeling in his gut even more.

"What are you thinking?" Sienna sounded both exhausted and anxious herself.

"I'm thinking that Anita—or Ruth, whatever you want to call her—isn't a victim here."

Sienna nodded, his revelation obviously not a surprise to her. "At least we have a name. Ruth Bolin." The Brightons had told them that before they left.

"Now let's just hope that's not an alias." Devin had already called in the lead to his colleague at the FBI. He hoped it would turn up something. "This still doesn't get us much closer to figuring out what's going on. Who's the man who tried to snatch Colby?"

"I have no idea. A friend of Anita's?"

"Maybe. Why try to snatch him? There's just so much that doesn't make sense."

"I agree."

He glanced in his rearview mirror and cringed.

There was a truck behind them. It had been there for the past several minutes, a subtle distance back—but Devin didn't want to take any chances.

"What is it?" Sienna asked, looking over her shoulder.

"Nothing to be concerned about. Not yet." He needed to know for certain that they were being followed before he alarmed Sienna.

Sienna turned back in her seat, but she still looked apprehensive as she crossed her arms over her chest and pressed her lips together. "It seems like everything concerns me lately."

"That's understandable." He glanced at her, deciding it was doing no good to keep his theory from her. "Someone is following us."

Sienna tightened her arms across her chest. "I hate this, Devin. All of it."

"I know. I do, too." He really did. He wanted it all to be over more than anyone.

He glanced in the mirror again.

There was the truck still, a decent distance behind them. But the vehicle was consistent. The driver didn't change lanes or back off or speed up. It kept pace with them.

They were definitely being followed.

Devin crossed two lanes and pulled off the interstate at the last minute. Cars honked in irritation at his unforeseen switch, but he didn't care. He wouldn't hit the other drivers. He just needed to change directions and see what play the other driver would make.

He glanced behind him again.

The truck was still there.

Somehow the driver had managed to get over across traffic behind him.

"Devin…" Sienna's voice pitched with fear.

"Just hold on. I've got this." He jammed on the accelerator. He was going to have to take more desperate measures here in order to lose this guy.

What did the person even want? For them to lead him back to Colby? To finish Devin and Sienna off before they could reveal what was really going on?

He didn't know.

He made a hard right at the end of the exit and bit back a frown.

This wasn't the exit he wanted. No, there was nothing here except for one gas station. That meant they'd be hitting some mountain roads here in a minute.

That was the last place they needed to be during a car chase.

Dear Lord, protect us.

He stayed on the main road for as long as he could, knowing that if he ventured off it would be even more dangerous.

But the truck was still there, and it wasn't backing off.

"What are we going to do, Devin?" Sienna asked.

"We've got to lose this guy somehow." His mind raced ahead, trying to figure out the best solution.

He was going to have to get off this road, he realized.

In front of him, there was nothing but a windy, narrow road filled with only a few lanes that led to houses. Here would be no way to escape.

And until he knew what the person following him wanted, he couldn't chance them coming face-to-face. Not with Sienna, anyway.

He didn't like how any of this was looking.

He turned right onto a smaller road. It was surrounded by trees on either side, and the mountain loomed around them.

No cliffs.

Not yet, at least.

But his SUV kicked into a higher gear as the incline increased.

He glanced at Sienna and saw her white-knuckled grip on the door handle.

"I'm going to get you out of this, Sienna," he told her. "I promise."

The truck remained behind them. But it was gaining speed.

Just what was this guy trying to do?

Devin had no idea.

As they rounded a bend, a mile up the mountain, the truck appeared again.

This time it was closer than ever.

As Devin pressed the accelerator harder, the truck nudged them.

They lurched forward.

Sienna let out a scream.

Devin's lungs tightened as he pushed the vehicle as fast as it could go.

Before they could gain any speed, the truck hit them again.

This time they lurched forward—and right into a rocky cliff.

Sienna blinked with confusion and glanced around her as time seemed suspended.

They'd just been hit.

And, in turn, they'd hit a cliff.

Her gaze jerked to Devin. He looked equally dazed but quickly snapped out of it.

"Are you okay?" he asked. Haze from the airbags filled the interior of the SUV, and the airbags themselves made everything around them seem otherworldly, as well as making it hard to see.

Sienna nodded. She thought she was fine. But how long would that be true? Where was the man who'd hit them?

She glanced behind her. Darkness stared back—night had fallen.

And the man was gone. The truck was gone.

But it couldn't be that easy…could it? Had he run them off the road just to leave?

"Come on." Devin grabbed her hand. "We need to move."

Before she could even catch her breath, he tugged her across the seat and out the driver-side door. Her own door wouldn't open. No, the impact of the crash had assured that.

Once they stood on the asphalt beside the car, Devin glanced around.

Sienna followed his gaze. That truck was nowhere in sight.

What was going on here? Had the truck just kept going? What sense did that make? There had to be more to this, part of the plan they weren't seeing yet.

And that made Sienna even more anxious.

"We need to take shelter until we figure this out," Devin said. "We can call for help after that. But it's getting late, and I don't like how any of this is playing out."

"Believe me. I don't, either."

He put his hand on her back and led her toward the woods in the distance. He was right. Being concealed there was better than being an open target on the road.

Especially since Sienna didn't think this was over yet.

They dodged past trees and bushes.

Normally, she found the Colorado landscape breathtaking. But right now, she couldn't observe it or revel in it. No, right now, she needed to move. As fast as possible.

Devin kept a hand on her back as they rushed deeper into the brush, guiding her as to where to go and pointing out hazards.

When they were far enough away that they could no longer see the road, they stopped. She gulped in deep breaths of air.

Devin didn't seem to relax, though. No, he glanced around, still on the lookout for danger.

Then he pulled out his phone.

He hit a few buttons before grimacing.

"What is it?" Sienna asked.

"There's no signal."

"So what are we going to do?"

"Go somewhere else where we can get a signal."

"Back toward the road?" she asked, her muscles tensing at the possibility.

Before Devin could answer, a sound cut through the stillness of the forest.

Gunfire.

Whoever had been driving that truck was now firing at them. Was the man hunting them? Was this all a big game to him?

"Get down!" Devin shielded Sienna with his own body. "We've gotta move."

He took her hand and pulled her toward the forest, deeper into the sinking darkness and farther away from everything that was familiar. They crouched, staying low and trying to remain out of sight.

Another gunshot rang out.

Sienna sucked in a breath. That one had been close. Too close.

She hadn't seen it, but she could sense that the bullet had whizzed by dangerously close.

"You okay?" Devin asked.

"I think so." As soon Sienna said the word, she felt something rip into her skin. She let out a yelp and sank to the ground.

No, get up, Sienna. Keep moving.

She tried to push herself up but couldn't. Her calf…

Devin knelt beside her. "Are you okay?"

She wanted to nod but couldn't. "I cut myself. I'm so sorry. I think a stick scratched me…"

"It's okay. We've got this." Using a pocket-knife, he ripped the bottom of his undershirt off and tied it around her leg. "This should stop the bleeding for now."

"Thank you."

Without hesitation, he lifted her into his arms and took off—slower this time. More carefully with her in his arms.

But at least they were moving farther from the gunman.

After what seemed like an hour—it was probably only twenty minutes—Devin found a craggy rock and ducked behind it. "Let's rest here for a minute."

"Do you think we lost him?" Sienna's breath now came out in a puff of icy air.

The nighttime could still be so cold here in the Rockies, even in the summer. The high elevation thinned the air, making it hard to breathe.

"I think we have. He'll have a harder time finding us in the darkness, at least."

She stared off into the distance. That's right. The darkness. It was all around them. She must have noticed it earlier, except she hadn't. She'd been so distracted and the darkness had fallen so gradually.

"So we wait?" she asked.

Devin glanced at her, his face grim. "So we wait."

SEVENTEEN

As Sienna shivered, Devin scooted closer. It was chilly out here in the craggy mountains. The boulder behind them felt like ice, and the air was brisk. And sitting on this rock, not knowing what was happening around them…it was unnerving.

He would guess they were four miles from the road. They'd mostly gone downhill, so heading back would be even harder. The good news was that he had his gun. The bad news was that Sienna was hurt.

He pulled out his phone and frowned. Still no signal.

They waited silently as the minutes ticked past. There was no sign that the man had found them.

After an hour, he felt like it was safe to begin moving again. It was too risky to walk back to his SUV. Between the terrain, the gunman and the cut on Sienna's leg, it was better if they stayed put—if possible.

But if they stayed here, they were going to need something to keep them warm. It was probably forty degrees out here, and neither Devin nor Sienna was dressed for the chilly weather.

If he was going to be proactive here, he had to get busy now.

Devin stood and began collecting dry sticks from the ground around them. The little cove they'd found beneath the boulder would be the perfect place to settle until the sun started to come up.

"What are you doing?" Sienna sat with a knee pulled to her chest, and exhaustion was written over her features. Every time she moved her leg, it was obvious she was in pain.

Devin wished there was something he could do to help her, but there wasn't. There was nothing other than this.

"I'm trying to find wood to start a fire," he said.

"Won't that attract the gunman's attention?"

"If he's still out here. But if he's not still out here and we don't start a fire, it's going to get cold. We can't risk walking any more tonight. It's too hard to see and with your injury…"

Sienna frowned. "I can't believe I didn't see that stick."

"The terrain is treacherous, even for seasoned mountain climbers. Don't beat yourself up."

"It's kind of hard not to when not watching my

step could get us killed." Sienna squeezed her eyes shut before dipping her head down into the crook of her arms, which rested on her knees.

Devin's heart twinged with compassion. He had the strange desire to reach over and try to offer Sienna some kind of comfort. But this wasn't the time. And it wasn't his place.

Though something strange had been happening to his heart lately. He wasn't sure what it was about Sienna, but she brought out feelings in him that he'd never thought he'd feel again.

And he didn't like it. He shoved those thoughts aside.

Once he collected all of the sticks, he put them together in a temporary fire pit. He then pulled out a flint and tried to start the fire. Yes, he'd been a Boy Scout. Those skills still came in handy.

A few moments later, he saw the first spark, and before long, the entire bundle was crackling in front of them.

Still on guard, he went back to sit by Sienna. He told himself he should sit somewhere else. Yet he couldn't seem to move.

"Life isn't fair sometimes, is it?" Sienna said, staring into the flames.

"No, it's not." He understood where she was coming from all too well.

"A two-year-old boy shouldn't have to go

through this," she continued. "I just wish that life worked the way we wanted it to, you know?"

"If life worked the way we wanted it to, then we'd never have the opportunity to grow. It's the trials that make us stronger." It was easier to say than it was to live.

"Who says we need to be strong? Why can't we just be happy and superficial?"

He glanced over at her, Sienna's words surprising him.

"I don't mean that," she muttered. "I just… I don't know. I don't know what I'm thinking. It's just tempting sometimes, isn't it?"

"I know what you're getting at, Sienna. But life is richer when we accept that there are going to be challenges."

Even as he said the words, he wasn't sure he'd lived that out. He'd spent a lot of time resenting the fact that he'd lost his wife and daughter. More than resenting it. He'd been angry. Angry at God. Angry at life.

He was just now starting to come out of the fog he'd been in for so long. And, in part, that was because of Sienna.

"He was stupid, you know," Devin said.

"What?" Sienna asked, surprise written across her face as she turned to look at him.

"Your fiancé. He was stupid for leaving you at the altar."

She let out a soft chuckle. "Yeah, I can't believe I didn't see that side of him before. But it's better that he realized he didn't love me before we got married rather than after."

"I can't argue with that. It's great that you can have a good attitude about it. But why did you really stay here? Was that the whole reason you gave me earlier?"

"What I said earlier was true. I'd already moved in. Signed a contract for my new job. I just felt like I should stay and see this through. I guess…well, I guess it was a matter of prayer and listening to this internal voice telling me this was where I should be."

"So it was a step of faith. Do you regret it?"

She shrugged. "It's hard to say. But most days, no. I've met a lot of great people, and I love my students."

"You obviously love Colby."

She smiled. "I do. I really do. He deserves a chance at life, you know."

"Yeah, I know." Their gazes caught, and Devin found himself leaning toward her. Drawn to her. Attracted to her.

No, that couldn't be right. He couldn't move on. To do so would be a travesty. It would be like leaving his wife and daughter in the past. Forgetting them. Forgetting how important they were to him.

So why did he want to kiss Sienna so badly?

As he looked at her, he saw the same desire in her eyes. She felt the same pull that he did.

What would it be like if he just let himself go? If he stopped worrying so much and instead embraced the fact that his future might have room for someone else? And that it was okay?

He reached for Sienna and skimmed his thumb along the edge of her cheek, then her jawbone.

"I'm sorry I acted like a jerk," he said.

Sienna blinked with surprise. "You acted like a jerk?"

"All those months of living beside each other, and I hardly ever spoke."

"Oh, back then." She smiled. "I'd say you've made up for it over the past couple of days. You've gone above and beyond, as a matter of fact."

"I hope so." He couldn't pull his eyes away. No, Sienna had the type of face and disposition that he wanted to study for hours upon hours.

His hand rested on her neck, he realized.

He reached forward with his other hand and slipped it around Sienna's waist.

She didn't object.

"Sienna?" he started, his throat achy with emotion.

"Yes?" She sounded breathless.

"You've really surprised—" Before he could finish the thought, he heard a twig snap in the distance.

Had the person trying to kill them come back?

Or it could be a bear. A mountain lion. There were so many dangers out here that he couldn't begin to name them all.

Instead, he jerked his hands back and pulled out his gun.

"What is it?" Sienna asked.

"Something—or someone—is out there. I need to figure out what."

Sienna pulled her knees to her chest, trying to make herself as small as possible there in the shadow of the boulder.

Please, Lord, protect us.

She watched as Devin slowly crept forward, using the trees for cover.

But it was so dark out here. It was so hard to see anything.

And her leg throbbed. Why did she have to cut it? What if that one mistake ended up costing them their lives? What would happen to Colby then?

She tried to put the thoughts out of her head. Instead, Sienna continued to watch everything going on around her.

If she saw something, she needed to signal to Devin that danger was approaching.

Sienna held her breath. Waiting. Anticipating.

Another twig cracked, followed by footsteps. Devin took off running after a fleeing figure in the distance.

Sienna pulled herself in even farther, wishing she could disappear. Wishing she could run after Devin and help. She didn't know what she wanted—only that she couldn't bear it if anyone got hurt.

The sounds of them running faded.

What was happening out there? Had Devin caught the man? Had the man caught him?

She closed her eyes and prayed more.

Thoughts of Colby rushed through her mind. Of Anita. Of their futures.

Her thoughts immediately shifted to the terrain in this area. With it being so dark outside, Devin could easily not see a cliff or other obstacles in his way.

Why did the thought of something happening to him make Sienna's chest ache so badly? In these two short days since they'd been thrown together, had she really started to care about him?

No, the idea was crazy.

Besides, even if that were true, it didn't mean Devin cared about her also.

Yet, he had almost seemed like he was about to kiss her. Sienna's heart pounded harder.

Had she been imagining things? Had the stress of the situation played with her mind?

She didn't know.

Sienna only knew she didn't want him to get hurt right now. That she couldn't handle the thought of it.

A twig snapped beside her. She gasped and looked up, fully expecting to see Devin.

Instead, a masked man stood there, pointing a gun toward her.

"Stand up. Make a sound, and I'll pull the trigger."

EIGHTEEN

Quietly, Devin cut through the dark forest, careful to watch his step. At any time the darkness could turn into a cliff. This place was beautiful—but perilous.

He'd lost the trail of the man who'd been lurking nearby.

Where had he gone?

Devin's guard was up as he scanned around him. Tall dark trees stared back, looming over him. Boulders stood guard. And there was darkness. Lots and lots of darkness.

That man could be anywhere.

And Devin could be in his crosshairs.

His spine clenched.

His gut told him something was wrong. Had this been a ploy to get him away from Sienna?

He had to get back to her. A bad feeling squeezed his gut.

Carefully, he traced his steps, still using the trees for cover. He had to make his way back to

Sienna—but he had to be careful about it. The last thing he needed was to lead the shooter right to her.

Devin paused behind a fir tree and glanced around. There was still no sign of the man. But Devin could see a faint spark from the fire he'd started through the foliage.

What if he had circled back around—back toward Sienna?

Devin's heart rate sped up, and he quickened his steps at the thought. He had to get back to her. Now.

With gun in hand, he pushed himself up the mountainside toward the location where he'd left Sienna. But just as he reached the area, he saw the shadowy figure. Standing next to Sienna. With a gun to her head.

Sienna's face was twisted with pain as the man gripped her arm and leered toward her.

He sucked in a deep breath as she let out a cry. No...

The fire illuminated the scene. The man beside Sienna wore a black ski mask, making it impossible to see any of his features. But it was definitely the same man Devin had encountered before.

"Put your gun down," the man ordered. He'd obviously been waiting for Devin to return. "Now. Otherwise I'll shoot her."

"Don't do anything drastic." Devin squatted

to the ground and placed his weapon there. "My gun is down. Let's talk about this."

"We do have a lot to talk about," the man growled. "Where's the baby?"

"He's somewhere safe." And Devin had no intention of telling him where.

"Where?" The man jerked Sienna until she let out a gasp.

Devin's heart hammered. No. Not Sienna.

He'd already lost two people he loved. He didn't want to lose Sienna, too. Not that he loved her. It was too early for that. But there was definitely the start of something there.

"It's not important," Devin said. This man couldn't take away his chance to explore that. Yet the reality remained that he could. Devin knew that all too well.

"It's important if I say it's important!" The man veered on the edge of desperation. His voice grew louder and more agitated. He jerked Sienna again, and his gun flew around wildly, the barrel no longer facing Sienna.

He wasn't a professional criminal, Devin realized. Not even an experienced one, for that matter. No, the man didn't have a plan. He only had his desperation and gut instinct.

Devin needed to use that knowledge to his advantage.

"Listen, we couldn't tell you anyway," Devin

said, his eyes remaining on the man's gun. "We'd have to take you there."

"Just give me the address. I'm not taking you anywhere."

If Devin gave him the address, he had a feeling this man would shoot both of them and go snatch Colby.

That couldn't happen.

Sienna let out another cry of desperation. Her eyes were wide with fear. The man had pulled her to her feet, but she hobbled in pain. Her leg obviously still hurt.

How was Devin going to get out of this one? He wasn't sure.

But he would come up with a plan. That was what he did. He planned. He executed. Nine times out of ten, he succeeded. This would not be that 10 percent.

"I can't give you the address," Devin said, inching closer. "We'd have to take you there."

"Do you think I'm stupid?" The man let out a bitter laugh.

"I'm just telling you the truth." Again, Devin paced a little closer, trying to become nearer to Sienna. All the while, he kept an eye on the man's gun. One wrong move, and it could be over for both him and Sienna.

"Give it to me or I'll shoot her!" The man jerked Sienna closer.

Sienna let out another cry.

The situation was escalating—the last thing Devin wanted.

"Okay, okay," Devin tamped the air with his hands. "Just don't hurt anyone. It's 23192 Issaquena Drive. It's in Denver."

The man paused, and Devin knew he was trying to remember the address Devin had spouted.

"Are you tricking me?" he asked.

"No," Devin said.

"Tell me the address again."

Devin repeated it.

"She's coming with me." The man jerked Sienna again, and pain rippled across her face.

Her leg.

Devin couldn't let this happen. The man couldn't go anywhere with Sienna. He'd never get her back alive.

As the man began backing away, Sienna still in a chokehold, Devin made a split-second decision.

In two seconds flat, he grabbed the spare gun he kept in his ankle holster, and he raised it toward the intruder.

As he did, a loud bang cut through the air, and time froze around him.

Sienna held her breath, unsure what had just happened as the sound echoed in her ears.

Someone had fired. But who? Where?

She waited for the pain. Or to see pain on Devin's face.

Instead, she froze and the world seemed to stand still around her.

Then the man behind her moaned and fell to the ground.

She gasped and hobbled away. As she got a good look at him, she saw something on his shoulder. Was that blood? It was too dark to tell.

Devin darted forward and snatched the gun off the man, who remained motionless.

"Good try, but he wasn't leaving with you," Devin said. "I was never going to let that happen."

"Is he…is he…dead?" Sienna asked.

Devin knelt beside him. "No, he hit his head when he fell. It must have knocked him out. That bullet only skimmed his shoulder. He'll be okay."

The next instant, Sienna fell into Devin's arms. It was like her bones had given out, and she could no longer hold herself up. Devin caught her and pulled her close. His scent—now familiar—brought a wave of comfort over her.

"It's okay, Sienna," he murmured. "It's going to be okay."

"What…what are we going to do?" She buried her face in his chest.

"First, we're going to find out who he is." Devin reached over and pulled the ski mask from his face.

Sienna studied the man's face. His broad nose. Big eyebrows. Thick jawline.

She waited for something to bring back an old memory, but it didn't. She'd never seen this man before.

"Do you recognize him?" she asked Devin.

"No, I don't. But we need to tie him up." Devin glanced around, searching for something they could use.

Sienna jerked her head back. "We're not going to take him with us?"

"He's injured. We'd have to drag him. And your leg is hurt. The journey would be nearly impossible. I'll call the police and tell them what happened. They'll pick him up." Devin pulled out his phone. "Unfortunately, there's no signal out here. I'll have to wait until I get back up the road."

"What do you need to tie him up with?" Sienna asked. "I'll help look."

"I'm going to have to use my shirt," he muttered. "There's nothing else."

He tugged off his undershirt, leaving his flannel shirt on. He then used his knife to cut the fabric into strips. Using those, he tied the man's arms and feet together, and then tied him to a tree.

"What should we do?"

"He's out cold. The best thing we can do is let the police question him."

"If you're sure." She hated to leave the man, but she understood Devin's reasoning.

Devin nodded. "Yeah, I'm sure. We need to have your cut looked at."

She winced, remembering her injury.

"Can you hold out one more moment?" he asked.

She nodded stiffly. She'd do whatever she had to do to get out of this alive…and to keep Colby safe.

Devin found the man's wallet in his pocket, along with his car keys. He slipped them into his own pocket before joining Sienna again.

Taking one last look at the man, he slipped an arm around Sienna's waist and began helping her back up the mountain. He was worried about her. Worried about how much blood she might be losing. Concerned for her level of anxiety right now.

They'd find answers later. Right now, Devin needed to make sure she was okay.

"I'm sorry you're in the middle of all this," Sienna told him, her voice soft and apologetic.

"None of this is your doing, Sienna."

"It feels like my fault." She gripped his waist and let out a groan as she marched on like a soldier.

"Well, feelings can be deceitful. You're just as much an innocent bystander as Colby."

"Maybe we should wait for that man to wake up and try to get some answers from him."

Devin had thought about that also. He desperately wanted answers. But… "I'm afraid you're going to bleed out, Sienna. We can't risk that. The man's not getting away. Not in his current state."

Sienna said nothing. Did she know how serious her injury might be? It was impossible to tell in the dark.

As they reached the top of the incline, a wind swept across them. They'd gotten out of the forest just in time. A storm was blowing in.

They couldn't take Devin's SUV. Not in its current condition—crushed against the side of the mountain with the airbags deployed.

But he did have the keys to the mystery man's truck.

He glanced around. A quad-cab truck was parked in front of Devin's. It was an older-model vehicle. That had to belong to the man in black.

He helped Sienna hop over to it and secured her in the passenger seat. He then climbed in himself and started the engine. He turned on the heat to warm them up.

The vehicle smelled like dirty shoes and rotting fast food. But it would be sufficient. Devin glanced at the gas gauge and saw the vehicle had a half a tank left. That would have to work.

"I'm going to take you to the hospital," he said.

Sienna swung her head back and forth. "It's too risky. Just go to a drugstore or a gas station and we'll get some supplies there. I'll be fine."

"I don't know, Sienna."

"I will be. Please. I just need to see Colby. To get a shower and a warm meal—preferably at the Jennings Center. With Colby."

"It's your call." He tossed the wallet he'd taken from the gunman into her lap. "See what you can find out about the man. In the meantime, I'm going to call the cops and have them pick this guy up."

But Devin didn't want one tragedy to turn into another. If they didn't take care of themselves, then they'd be in no position to see this mission through to completion. He only hoped there was a resolution to all of this…and soon.

NINETEEN

"Justin Henderson is his name," Sienna said, staring at the man's photo on his driver's license.

She and Devin headed down the road, leaving the nightmare from the forest behind them.

She couldn't think about it too hard. If she did, she'd want to retreat or hyperventilate. Instead, she tried to focus on finding answers within this man's wallet.

She stared at Justin Henderson's picture. The man was tall with unkempt blond hair and a broad build. In the picture, he almost had the expression of a schoolboy. It was halfway innocent and halfway rambunctious. But he didn't scream criminal.

Still, that didn't mean anything. It just surprised her. Sienna had expected the person in the photo to have a hardened expression. To look evil and heartless.

"I know we saw the man's face in the woods. But now that you see a more clean-cut photo of him, do you recognize him at all?" Devin asked, glancing over as he drove down the road.

"No, I've never seen him before. His license says he's from Utah."

"That's where the Brightons lived. Maybe we're finding answers. Answers I don't want to hear, but answers nonetheless." He gripped the steering wheel as they traveled down the road, headed toward the nearest town. "Anything else of significance?"

Sienna shuffled through a couple of credit cards and some faded receipts for fast food, but those things told her nothing. "No. Not really."

"Look in his glove compartment."

She opened the compartment and shuffled through the papers there. There was an owner's manual for the truck, a couple of parking tickets and some hand sanitizer.

"There's really nothing in here that tells me anything." She leaned back. "Sorry."

"Let me call my contact back and give him the name." He hit a button on his phone, and Detective Jenson's voice came through the speakers.

Devin relayed the information to him.

"Good work," Jenson said. "Our guys should be getting to the area where you left the gunman. I'll let you know what we find out."

"Thanks, Jenson."

At some point since they'd left, trembles had begun to overtake Sienna. All of her adrenaline had come to a head, and her body was now catching up with all of her mental stress.

Devin glanced over and did a double take at her. "Hey, you okay?"

She folded her hands beneath her, trying to do something to cover up her reaction. "Yeah, I'll be fine."

"It was scary back there. You did fine." He reached over and grabbed her hand. As he did, the lights of a nearby store came into eyesight in the distance.

"Thank you. I just…" She remembered the feel of the gun against her. How her life flashed before her eyes.

Again.

Twice in two days.

The nightmare felt surreal…but the cut on her leg and her pounding headache proved that it was all too real.

Devin pulled into the parking lot of a gas station and put the vehicle in Park. As he did, a smattering of rain hit the windshield. A storm was definitely blowing in.

The glow of the gas station offered just enough light in the truck, and stopping gave them a moment to catch their breath.

Devin turned toward Sienna, and his fingers brushed her jaw. His eyes looked tender and raw as he stared at her.

"It's okay to be scared, Sienna."

The gentleness of his words made tears rush to her eyes. Sienna hadn't realized just how alone she'd felt over the past few months. She hadn't realized how good it felt to have someone who actually cared. Who had her back. Who looked at her like this.

Devin wiped away the moisture on her cheeks using the crook of his fingers. His eyes assessed her face with such concern that long-dormant emotions rose in her.

"Sienna…"

"I'm a mess. I know." She hated for him to see her like this.

He pulled her closer until her head hit his chest—his solid chest. She didn't hold back. No, she rested in his embrace and let herself cry for a moment. It felt good to not hold back and to somehow express all the wild fears that dwelled in her. Tears expressed what words couldn't. Her mother had often said that, and there was a lot of wisdom there.

Sienna drew back, trying to compose herself, and looked up at Devin, ready to say thanks. Instead, their gazes caught.

She saw the same attraction in Devin's eyes that she felt toward him also.

Slowly, he leaned in, and his lips met hers. Fire sparked between them, and Devin slid closer. Sienna felt herself melting as the kiss deepened.

Then, as quickly as it had started, Devin

jerked back and looked away, running a hand over his face. "I'm sorry, Sienna. I shouldn't have done that."

Sienna's heart slammed into her chest. Devin was sorry? For kissing her?

All the good feelings that had swollen inside her shriveled to dust. She drew back, feeling the sting of rejection all over again.

Memories of being left at the altar slammed into her mind with such intensity that she flinched.

"Sienna..." Devin started, reaching for her.

She raised a hand to stop him. "No, no. You're right. That was a bad idea. A really bad idea."

"That's not what I meant—"

"You don't have to explain, Devin." *I'm always a mistake.* She wasn't sure where the thought had come from. Maybe it had always been there, lingering in the back of her mind. The lie that she wasn't enough. Or desirable. Or lovable.

Jackson hadn't said it, but his actions had.

And that kiss seemed to prove it all true.

Devin's eyes looked tortured as he pulled his gaze up to meet hers. "Really, Sienna. It's just that..."

He couldn't finish the thought. She didn't even care what kind of explanation he had. She'd been a fool to ever let that hope grow inside her. What was she thinking?

"My leg is hurting. Why don't we just forget

that happened and stay focused on the mission at hand here?"

Devin looked away and nodded. "Let's revisit this later, okay?"

She didn't say anything.

After a moment of silence, he shoved something into her hand. She looked down and saw a…gun. Sienna's heart rate ricocheted again.

"What's this for?"

"You know how to shoot one of these?" Devin asked.

She nodded quickly, apprehensively. "My dad taught me, but it's been a while."

"Hold on to this, just in case. I'm going to run inside and get the supplies we need. Then I'll be back to get some gas. You going to be okay?"

"I'll be fine." Yet the metal of the weapon seemed to burn into her hands. Could she really pull the trigger if she had to? She wasn't sure.

Devin disappeared, leaving the darkness to surround her and her only company to be loneliness.

As Devin escaped to a dingy bathroom inside the gas station, he tried to regain control of his emotions. Yet his mind swirled like it hadn't done in years.

He splashed some water onto his face.

Kissing Sienna had been amazing. More than

amazing. It had stirred something in him that had seemed long dormant.

But as soon as the bliss ended, the truth slammed into his mind.

He couldn't do this to his wife. No, her memory deserved to be preserved. He couldn't forget Grace and how special what they'd had was. Being with Sienna somehow felt like a betrayal.

He glanced in the mirror. A ragged man stared back. It wasn't even his appearance that made him look that way. Sure, he was dirty and disheveled right now. But it was the haggard look in his eyes that said it all.

He raked a hand through his hair before stepping out. He went to the aisle where the first aid supplies were located and began looking for what he needed.

But the image of Sienna slammed into his mind again. How hurt she'd looked. Bewildered. How she'd tried to pull herself together like a soldier.

As he grabbed some water bottles, he glanced out the window. He saw Sienna there in the truck, staring out the window.

He'd never meant to hurt her like that. Never. Yet the woman had captured a piece of his heart. It seemed so unlikely. So against all the odds.

But no doubt about it—Sienna was special. Beautiful inside and out. Kind.

The fact she was still single seriously blew his

mind. She looked like she was made for family life. To be caring and nurturing.

It didn't matter. None of it mattered. What mattered right now was buying what he needed and getting back out to her. They had to get away from danger and find some answers.

He only hoped Detective Jenson would be able to break the will of Justin Henderson. Maybe he would crack and tell the police what was really going on here.

Then Colby could be safe. He and Sienna could return to their normal lives.

Would that normal life include pretending Sienna didn't exist? Could he ever go back to that?

He couldn't see it happening. No, not now that he knew Sienna and how special she was.

I'm sorry, Grace. You'll always be my love.

Yet something was changing inside him, wasn't it?

He took his first aid items, water and some crackers to the cashier. After paying, he made his way back out to the truck.

His heart quickened when he saw Sienna again.

He should have thought about it before it he kissed her. Thought about how much he could end up hurting her. Because that was the last thing he needed.

Just as he climbed into the truck, his phone rang.

It was Jenson.

He put the phone to his ear. "What's going on?"

"Devin, we're here at the site you told us about. There's no one here."

His muscles stiffened. "You can't be at the right area then. We left this guy tied to a tree."

"We can see where he was. The ties are still here, as well as blood. But the man is gone."

Devin shook his eye. "There's no way the man could have gotten away. He was too injured to break free and make his way out of the forest."

"We're not sure what happened. We just know he's gone. I thought you'd want to know."

Devin ended the call and leaned back, his thoughts racing. How could that have happened? And what did that mean for him and Sienna now?

TWENTY

"I just don't understand." Sienna let her head fall against the seat behind her as she replayed what Jenson had said. "How did that man get away? We left him tied up."

Devin shook his head, looking equally confused. "I have no idea. I'm just as surprised as you."

Sienna took a long sip of the water that Devin had brought her. She was chilly. She'd love nothing more than a nice warm blanket and some Colby cuddles.

Maybe she'd get those things.

Soon enough.

"He must be working with someone."

"I'm inclined to agree," Devin said. "That's the only way he could have gotten away."

"So was Anita lurking nearby the whole time? Is she the only one, or is there someone else, even?"

"Those are all great questions. We don't have any of those answers yet, though."

She lowered her head, feeling a headache coming on. As she shifted, her leg throbbed again. Why did it feel like everything was falling apart? Like every aspect of her life was in turmoil right now?

"Let me treat your cut," Devin said. "Hold tight."

Before Sienna could say anything, he was out of the car and opening her door. Before she could even move, he took her leg and carefully angled it out the door where he could see it in the light more.

Her skin burned at his touch.

Why did she have to react like that? She needed to get the man out of her system. But first she had to make sure Colby was safe. She could push through working with Devin until then. As soon as it was over, they could both go back to acting like the other didn't exist.

Except…could they?

Devin eased the leg of her jeans up higher and visibly cringed when he saw her cut. "This is deeper than I thought."

She gritted her teeth, trying not to show how much it hurt. She couldn't look herself. She already felt woozy. "Yeah, I know."

"I'm going to clean it. It won't feel good."

Her fingers dug into the seat as she anticipated the coming pain. "Thanks for the heads-up."

He twisted the top off a bottle of water and

poured the liquid over her cut, and pain sizzled through her. She squeezed her eyes shut.

"Don't forget to breathe," Devin said.

"Oh, I'm breathing. If I wasn't breathing, I wouldn't feel this," she said through gritted teeth.

She opened her eyes and saw a brief smile feather Devin's features. "I suppose you're right. I just don't want you passing out."

He blotted the moisture on her leg with some gauze. Then he put some butterfly bandages across her cut. Eight bandages all together.

"We should still get this checked out," Devin said, easing the leg of her jeans back down. "I think you need stitches."

"Let's see how this works first."

His eyes met hers. "You have a stubborn streak, I see."

"No, I just have priorities."

He leaned closer, as if forgetting his earlier hesitancy. "Remember, it's like putting the oxygen mask on yourself first and then your child, just like they tell you on airplanes. I used to have to remind my wife of that also." His voice cracked.

His wife. Was that what this was about? Was Devin not ready to move on yet?

Sienna couldn't even imagine his pain and grief. Losing a spouse and a child would be devastating for most. For some, it might derail them permanently. Either way, it had to be hard to move on.

Devin patted her uninjured leg as he stood in front of her. "You should be good for now. We should probably get moving."

"Don't forget we need gas."

"Of course." He climbed back in and pulled up to a pump.

As he began to fill the tank, Sienna's gaze traveled across the lot. A car sat in the corner of the lot near the dumpster.

She squinted. Had it been there before?

Sienna had been trying to keep an eye on her surroundings, but she didn't remember seeing it. The placement was odd, especially when there were parking spots closer to the door.

It was too dark to be sure, but were there two people sitting inside? She thought she saw the silhouettes.

Could this be Anita, and Justin Henderson?

Her heart rate quickened.

Maybe she was reading too much into this. Maybe they were just two travelers taking a break from a long drive.

Still, her gaze wouldn't leave the vehicle as her mind raced.

Devin climbed back in and glanced at her. "What's wrong?"

She told him about the car.

Devin's jaw tightened. "Let's go find out what's going on."

Before she could say anything, he put the truck in Drive and headed directly toward the mystery vehicle.

Devin's anticipation grew with every passing second.

Who was in that vehicle?

It had to be Anita and Justin. Had Anita been in the woods also? Had she untied Justin and helped him back to her vehicle? It seemed like a good possibility. And now the two of them followed Devin and Sienna here.

Just before he reached it, the car squealed away and onto the highway.

Devin jammed on the accelerator, taking off after them. "Your seat belt is on, right?"

Sienna looked down at her lap and nodded, her eyes wide. "Yeah, I'm good."

"Then hold on."

He stayed on the tail of the vehicle, determined not to lose it. But the driver kept a quick pace, even around the breakneck turns on the road.

He didn't recognize the vehicle, and it had Utah plates. There appeared to be two people inside. He mentally ticked off the facts.

This definitely had something to do with Colby. Otherwise, why would these people be running right now?

The car merged onto the interstate.

Thankfully, it wasn't busy at this time of night. But Devin had to choose wisely. The last thing he needed was for someone else to get hurt during this chase. That wasn't the way he wanted things to work.

"How long are we going to follow them?" Sienna asked, her face as white as her knuckles as she gripped the door handle.

"Until we know who's inside. It's time to put an end to this."

"What if they just keep going until they run out of gas?"

"Then we could be following them for hours. I'm not letting them out of my sight, though. Whoever is in that car has the answers we need. We've got to catch them."

"They could be dangerous."

"You're right. But we'll be careful."

They settled in to following the car. Devin had a full tank of gas, and he was in this. When the car stopped, he would be there to confront the driver. He couldn't let them get away.

Sienna cleared her throat, her anxiety seeming to die down some. "Why'd you become an FBI agent, Devin? Talk to me. Distract me from all these other thoughts I'm having. Please."

"Because I've always liked to fight for what was right, from standing up for the neighborhood nerd when bullies came after him to tracking down the person who stole my best friend's dog."

"Sounds noble. Do you miss working?"

He stayed on the car, willing to play this out for however long necessary. "I do. But I think I'm ready to go back. I've moved beyond burying myself in my work to deal with my pain."

"That's good to know."

"I guess I walked away with this feeling of how unfair life was. How unfair it was that Willow would never get the chance to grow up and have dreams. That my wife and I wouldn't grow old together. For my entire life, everything has gone according to plan."

"And then it didn't."

"And then it didn't."

"When do you go back?" she asked softly.

"I'm not sure. I was supposed to go in next week to talk things over with the director."

"Do you think you're ready?"

"I do." Even as Devin said the words, he remembered the strong guilt he'd felt after kissing Sienna. Did that mean he wasn't ready to go back? To resume life? Or was it the painful burst of emotion one felt before a major life change—a last goodbye of sorts to the things that had been holding him back? He didn't know. "Most of the time I do, at least."

"I know this isn't the same, Devin, but I lost my mom when I was eight. I never thought I would get over it. And I didn't. I just learned to live with it. I learned to keep a piece of her in my heart always. I know I'll never see her again on this earth, but she will always be a part of me."

"You're right, Sienna. It's just—" Before he could finish his thought, the car he was following pulled off at an exit. "What is this guy doing?"

"I guess we're about to find out."

He watched as the car turned right at the bottom of the exit, pulled to the side of the road and stopped.

He held his breath.

What now?

He hoped things didn't turn ugly.

TWENTY-ONE

Sienna stayed in the car, just as Devin directed her to do. But she could hardly breathe as she waited to see what happened.

She fully expected for someone to step out of the car they'd been following with a gun in hand and for a shootout to begin.

Instead, the doors to the other car opened. Two people stepped out with their hands raised. They turned toward Devin, the headlights of the truck illuminating them.

Sienna sucked in a deep gasp of air.

The Brightons.

The *Brightons* had followed them? Were they somehow involved in this?

She shook her head, unable to make sense of things.

When she saw Devin lower his gun, Sienna stepped from the vehicle and cautiously walked toward them. She strained to hear the conversation.

"Please, don't shoot," Joyce said, tears streaming down her face. "We didn't mean any harm."

Devin's entire body looked stiff and ready to act, if necessary. "Why were you following us?"

"Because we thought you knew something about Liam." George glanced mournfully at his wife. "We thought maybe you could lead us to him."

"We told you we'd let you know," Devin said. He didn't sound angry, but he didn't sound pleased, either.

"Yes, but we've heard that before," Joyce said, lowering her hands slightly. "We've been left in the dark before. We just want answers."

Sienna could only imagine. She'd probably do the same thing in their shoes. "I understand that this must be difficult for you. But we're not intentionally leaving you in the dark. We don't want to get your hopes up, either."

"I'd welcome some hope right about now." Joyce's voice cracked. "I don't think you understand the agony we've been in. Nothing's been the same without Liam. And nothing will be."

Again, Sienna's heart panged with grief for the couple.

Devin pressed his lips together, his thoughts obviously heavy as he weighed his options. "Look, there's another case we're following. There's a baby involved who matches Liam's description."

Joyce let out a gasp.

Devin raised a hand, trying to slow her thoughts. "We don't know that he's Liam, though. That's why we didn't want to tell you. We're trying to be cautious here."

"But it could be Liam?" Joyce's voice lilted with hope and her eyes were wide.

"We're trying to figure it out." Devin's voice was low and easy—not making promises, but not a coldhearted professional, either. "But, in the meantime, the best thing you can do is return home. We're dealing with some dangerous people. We don't believe they'll hurt Liam. But they will hurt anyone who gets in their way."

George stepped closer, wringing his hands together. "Is Liam in danger?"

Devin stole a quick glance at Sienna before responding. "If this baby is Liam, then he's somewhere safe and unreachable right now. We're trying to keep it that way."

Tears poured down both Joyce and George's faces as they hugged each other. Sienna really hoped—and prayed—that their hearts didn't break again. She felt certain that Colby was theirs, but there were still a lot of obstacles they needed to conquer to confirm that and before Colby could go back to them. Namely, they had to keep Anita away.

"Please, take us to see him," George said.

He looked desperate. Sienna couldn't describe it other than the look in his eyes—it was heart wrenching.

"Please," George said.

Sienna glanced at Devin and saw the agony on his face. He wanted to alleviate this couple's grief. But it wasn't time yet.

There were too many unknowns, too many dots to connect. But there were getting close.

"We can't do that," Devin said. "Please understand that the situation is complicated. Give us another day to figure things out."

"A day will feel like a year to us," Joyce said. "You have no idea."

"Please." Devin's voice held an edge of desperation. "I know it's hard. I do. But I just need a little more time. I don't want to act prematurely."

"You don't understand." Joyce's face crumpled into a mess of emotions and grief. "You don't know what it's like to lose a child like this!"

Devin's face tightened again, and Sienna put her hand on his back, trying to comfort him.

"I understand more than you'd think," he finally said. "Every day, I'd give anything to get my daughter back. I miss her every single day. I think about her. I wonder what she would be like. So I do understand."

George and Joyce hugged each other, both crying. Finally, they pulled apart, and Joyce nodded while dabbing her eyes with a crumpled tissue.

"We'll wait," she said, her voice trembling.

"I'm sorry for any trouble we might have caused. We just…we just want answers."

"That's all we want," Devin said. "Believe me, it's all we want also."

Back in the truck, Devin's heart felt like it had been crushed.

Seeing the couple's grief. Understanding their loss. Being unable to offer any comfort… it nearly broke him. He wanted nothing more than to give them good news, but he knew he couldn't. Not yet.

Sienna reached for his arm, her eyes wide and compassionate. "I'm sorry, Devin."

He nodded stiffly and took several deep breaths. "It's okay. It's not your fault."

"I know that had to be difficult."

"It comes with the territory, I suppose." He leaned his head against the seat behind him a moment, a headache coming on. Just as he did that, rain began splattering the window again. They'd hit patches of the storm earlier, but soon it would be fully upon them.

It was already 3:00 a.m. They were still two and a half hours from where they'd left Colby. And both Devin and Sienna were on their last legs.

Sienna was injured. They were both exhausted. Hungry. In need of some rest.

Yet the clock was still ticking. The urgency of the situation hadn't waned.

Colby's life was in danger. The Brightons were waiting to find out if Colby was theirs.

There just wasn't any time to rest.

"What are you thinking?" Sienna asked softly.

"I'm thinking we need to get back to Colby."

"And then what? How do we find Anita? How do we find this Justin guy?"

"You know, maybe the best thing we can do is wait for the police to find answers. Maybe we should just keep an eye on Colby and let everyone else do their jobs. We're targets right now, and I'm not sure there's anything else we can do other than wait."

Sienna nodded. "Okay then. That's what we'll do. For a little while, at least."

"We should get back as soon as we can. We're not safe out here."

But before he could take off, his phone rang. It was Jenson. He'd probably gotten less sleep than they had.

"By the way, I just did a search on that Ruth woman you gave us the name for. The one who worked at the day care. We didn't get any hits on her name. It was probably an alias. But we found something in Anita's house that didn't make sense to us, and we decided to dig a little

"That's right. My guys are working on it. You know as well as I do that these things don't happen as quickly in real life as they do on TV."

"I understand that, but listen. Can you run the dental records on the body and compare them to a reporter named Lisa Daniel?"

Sienna drew in a deep breath. Lisa? Could Lisa be dead?

She remembered the pictures of Lisa. The woman was about the same size and height as Anita. Could it be...?

She didn't even want to think about it. Didn't want to think about what turn of events might have led to a tragedy like that. Or who was responsible. Because if that body wasn't Anita's, did that mean that... Anita was behind this?

It was definitely a possibility.

As Devin ended the call, Sienna turned toward him, wanting to see his expression as she asked her next question. "Where did that theory come from?"

"Lisa Daniel disappeared two days ago—soon after the body was discovered dead in the woods. The timeline, unfortunately, fits. I don't want to believe it's true, but..."

"I hate this, Devin." A shiver went down Sienna's spine at the coldheartedness of it all. "I hate the devastation and destructiveness of what's happened."

"It's something I've had to come to terms with

deeper. It turns out that Anita is actually Angela Williams."

Devin sat up straighter. "And who is Angela Williams?"

Sienna leaned closer, trying to hear.

"Angela Williams was in the army. But she was in an accident that caused her to have both physical and mental issues."

"Can you expound?"

"She was injured in a training exercise. She fell from a wall she was trying to climb, and she landed hard. She injured her pelvis, and doctors told her she'd never have a baby."

"Wow," Devin muttered.

"She didn't recover well—physically or emotionally. The military kicked her out—dishonorably discharged her. She's originally from Kansas, but she lived several places before moving to Utah. She disappeared from there six months ago and showed up in Colorado with another identity."

"That's very useful," Devin said. "Do you have any more information about the man who's with her? Justin Henderson."

"We're still running all the information on him. It does appear that Justin Henderson is his real name. He has a rocky past, including jail time for assault on two different occasions.

"Good to know." It also confirmed what Devin already knew—the man was dangerous.

"It looks like he was a bouncer at a club in Utah. I'd guess that's where he and Angela met. You can probably fill in the rest of the details just as easily as I can."

"If you learn anything else, please let me know."

"Will do, Matthews."

Devin hung up and exchanged a look with Sienna.

A woman who'd gone crazy after learning she couldn't have a baby. A man with a violent criminal record. And a baby in the crosshairs.

He was determined this story would have a happy ending. He just wasn't sure what path he had to take to get there.

TWENTY-TWO

The pounding rain and occasional thunder seemed to match Sienna's mood as she processed everything Devin had told her. Thankfully, they were only about thirty minutes away from the Jennings Center now, and she'd be able to hold Colby for herself—and maybe get some pain medication to ease the throbbing in her leg.

She hated to admit it, but she felt a little sorry for Anita. Or should she refer to her as Angela? Sienna didn't know. She only knew the whole situation was twisted and messed up.

And, even as more answers poured in, Sienna still didn't understand why she'd been dragged into this. What could Anita possibly have to gain by asking Sienna to watch Colby? What had been so important that the woman had left Colby behind?

"People will go to desperate lengths to get what they want, won't they?" Devin said, his voice matching the cadence of the windshield wipers as they lazily sloshed back and forth. It was almost like he could read her thoughts.

Sienna turned her gaze away from the window for long enough to glance at him. "They will. Even if it means committing a crime."

"I suppose our minds and thoughts get twisted, sometimes. We get fixated on how we think things should be instead of taking what we've been handed."

Sienna wondered if there was a deeper meaning behind his words. Was he talking about himself as well? They'd both been in situations where life hadn't gone as they planned. He was right— it was always a choice how to respond to things.

"I suppose that's true," Sienna said. "But, you know, I'd always thought there was something off about Anita. Despite that, I tried to be nice, and I scolded myself for being judgmental. If I'd kept my distance, maybe none of this would have happened."

Devin reached over and rested his hand on her knee, offering her a moment of comfort. "She would have found someone else, Sienna. These people always do. And if she found someone else, she may have gotten away with this. She probably didn't anticipate you'd be such a fighter. Everything happens for a reason."

Everything happens for a reason. Sienna believed that. Now she needed to live like she believed it. She'd been put in the position for a reason. Much like Esther, she knew that sometimes a person's position in life happened for such a time as this. She couldn't fail now.

She let out a long breath, trying to think everything through. Until she had more answers, she wouldn't be able to stop. "We don't even know if Anita is still alive. I mean, sure, that body was found with her necklace. But Anita could have staged it."

Devin frowned and took a long sip of water. "I have a feeling that wasn't Anita. I have a feeling that body was just another way of throwing us off their trail."

"If not Anita, then who?" Sienna ate another peanut butter cracker, hoping it might make her feel less jittery. But the sick feeling remained in her gut as the gravity of the situation hit her.

Devin grimaced. "Now that you mention it, I have an idea that I need to call Jenson about. I need him to look into a theory for me—even though I desperately hope I'm wrong about it."

What was he talking about? Sienna braced herself as she waited to find out.

He put his phone on speaker as he dialed. Jenson answered a moment later.

"Jenson, that body you found—the one burned in the woods," Devin started.

"What about it?" Jenson asked.

"You haven't had any luck identifying it yet, correct?"

"That's right. My guys are working on it. You know as well as I do that these things don't happen as quickly in real life as they do on TV."

"I understand that, but listen. Can you run the dental records on the body and compare them to a reporter named Lisa Daniel?"

Sienna drew in a deep breath. Lisa? Could Lisa be dead?

She remembered the pictures of Lisa. The woman was about the same size and height as Anita. Could it be…?

She didn't even want to think about it. Didn't want to think about what turn of events might have led to a tragedy like that. Or who was responsible. Because if that body wasn't Anita's, did that mean that… Anita was behind this?

It was definitely a possibility.

As Devin ended the call, Sienna turned toward him, wanting to see his expression as she asked her next question. "Where did that theory come from?"

"Lisa Daniel disappeared two days ago—soon after the body was discovered dead in the woods. The timeline, unfortunately, fits. I don't want to believe it's true, but…"

"I hate this, Devin." A shiver went down Sienna's spine at the coldheartedness of it all. "I hate the devastation and destructiveness of what's happened."

"It's something I've had to come to terms with

as an FBI agent. We live in a fallen world full of sin. The consequences of sin…they're hard to swallow sometimes."

"Hard to swallow? I can't swallow them. Not at all. They cause me choke."

"And rightfully so. You have a pure heart. Always keep that, Sienna. Always."

His words warmed her. Funny how far the two of them had come over the past few days—from not speaking or really even liking each other, to finding support in the other's presence.

Devin pulled onto the lonely road that headed toward Rick and Trina's compound. They were almost there. The end was almost in sight.

And soon, Sienna would hold Colby and see for herself that he was okay.

The road was isolated, surrounded by trees and nothing else. Sienna would guess that the Jennings Center had purchased a lot of the surrounding land for privacy purposes. But something about the desolation made her shiver.

Rain still pounded the roof of the car when Devin threw on the brakes. The truck's headlights illuminated something in front of them.

A tall fir tree had come down across the road, blocking it from being passable—at least, that's how it looked.

Had the storm done this?

Or had *someone* done it?

Someone like Anita or Justin?

Sienna didn't know, but she didn't like the possibilities before her. Especially since those possibilities kept her away from Colby.

Devin blanched when he saw the blockade in front of him. The fir tree was tall and long, and it looked like it had been dying for a long time. All it had needed was a subtle push to send the brittle trunk toppling across the road.

"You've got to be kidding me," Devin muttered. "Stay here."

He climbed out and went to inspect the damage himself.

He didn't know what he hoped to find or prove by coming out here. Because the tree was clearly all the way across the road. It was big. Heavy. Impossible to move or get past.

Cold rain pounded him as he stared at it a moment.

There was no way to get around, he realized. The edges of the road were not only covered by the tree, but they were also steep—too steep to drive around.

He gazed in the distance as thunder rumbled overhead and lightning flashed in the sky.

Considering their already challenging day, this ending shouldn't be unexpected. It was, however, frustrating.

They were probably a good five-or ten-minute drive away from Rick and Trina's still. That would equal at least an hour of walking, maybe more, especially because of Sienna's hurt leg.

He could call his friend—he knew Rick wouldn't mind. But it was four in the morning.

Devin sighed. Out of curiosity, he walked toward the base of the tree to see what had happened. It had been a rainy spring, so the ground was moist and soft. Trees being uprooted wasn't entirely abnormal.

But he wouldn't take anything at face value right now—not when he considered everything that happened.

As he reached the base of the tree, he paused.

There was a mark on the tree where the bark had been scraped away by something.

He stepped closer.

Something glinted in the woods in the distance.

Was that...

He inched nearer, his nerves on edge.

It was just as he thought.

A car.

A maroon car with a smashed-in bumper.

This was the car the man had jumped into when escaping from Lisa Daniel's place.

It had somehow run off the road, hit this tree and knocked it into the road.

The direction of everything was messed up, though.

Then he realized that this hadn't been a casual accident. No, someone had veered off the road on purpose, lined up their car perfectly and hit that tree to purposefully fall across the road.

His pulse spiked.

That meant trouble was close.

Really close.

He had to get Sienna.

Now.

TWENTY-THREE

Sienna heard the door open beside her. Heard the pounding rain. Felt the cold sweep of air from outside.

Where had Devin gone? He'd disappeared into the woods, and she hadn't seen him emerge. Then again, the rain was so heavy it was blinding.

She glanced over and sucked in a deep breath.

Devin hadn't gotten in the truck.

No, a masked person had.

A masked person with a gun.

The gunman pulled the mask off and…

"Anita?" Sienna asked, her voice nearly breathless.

This wasn't the same Anita who'd been a quirky, chatty teacher assistant. No, this Anita looked crazy and unhinged.

"You couldn't have made this a little easier on me?" Anita muttered.

"Anita," Sienna said. "What are you doing? There's got to be a better way than this."

"Sorry you got pulled into this," Anita said. "But there was no other way."

"Colby isn't your child, Anita. He belongs to the Brightons, and they miss him terribly. How could you do this to another person? How could you rip their child from their arms?"

Anita sneered. "I don't have time to talk about that now. Now, I have other matters to attend to. If you don't cooperate, your boyfriend is going to die."

She stepped out of the car and jerked her gun toward the woods, where Devin emerged.

Sienna's heart pounded in her throat. Just how was this going to play out?

She had no idea.

She only prayed no one would get hurt.

"Put your gun down. Now!" Anita ordered.

Devin did as she asked, his hands in the air.

Sienna saw it all playing out in the headlights, like this was some kind of theatrical performance. Only it was anything but.

"Anita, let's not end things like this," Devin said.

"I'm calling the shots here. I have been from the start. Now climb into the driver's seat so we can all talk. Make any unexpected moves, and I'll shoot. Don't think I won't."

"Let's all stay calm." Devin climbed into the

truck and glanced at Sienna, as if making sure she was unharmed.

Anita climbed into the back, her gun still bobbing back and forth between the two of them. "Now, here's what's going to happen. And it's the only way things are going to happen. Understand?"

Neither Devin nor Sienna said anything.

"I said, do you understand?" Anita shouted.

"Yes, we understand," Devin said. "Maybe we'd understand better if you put the gun down. It's hard to concentrate."

"Like I said, I'm calling the shots here, so stop talking!" Anita's voice continued to get faster and louder. "You're going to do exactly what I say. Devin, Mr. FBI Agent…you're going to walk into that compound at the end of this lane, and you're going to get Colby. You're going to bring him to me."

"I can't do that, Anita. You know I can't."

"You will! Do you know why? Because if you don't, I'll kill Sienna." She jammed the gun into Sienna's head. "Do you understand that?"

Sienna gasped, and her body froze. Just one pull of the trigger, and it would all be over. Her heart pounded in her ears at the thought.

"There's got to be a different way of doing this," Devin said. "Can't we just talk it through—"

"There will be no talking! I already have this

all worked out, and I need you to do what I say. It's not complicated. You just have to listen."

"Okay, okay," Devin said. "We all just need to stay calm."

He glanced at Sienna, and she could see the emotions in his eyes. His worry about her. His concern over the situation. Over Colby.

"Please stop trying to call the shots here," Anita said, growing more agitated with each turn of the conversation. "No opinions are needed. No feedback. No advice. Just do what I say."

"Okay," Devin said. "So I go get Colby. I bring him back. And you release Sienna. Is that correct?"

"Yes. Finally, you're listening."

"And if I don't…"

"Then Sienna dies," Anita growled.

"It's going to take me a while to walk to the Jennings Center."

"You have two hours. That's it. You're fit. You can handle it."

"I have to get past the tree. In the rain. Then past security. I look like a wreck. I'm not even sure my friends will trust me enough in this state to hand Colby over, especially when they hear I don't have a vehicle."

"Then you'll have to think of a way to convince them. Why are we still discussing this? The clock starts now. In two hours, Sienna dies, and I have to take matters into my own hands. It will involve more people dying."

"Okay, okay," Devin said. "I'm going."

"One more thing," Anita said. "Give me your cell."

Devin frowned and handed the woman his phone. With one hand on the door handle, he glanced at Sienna again, his eyes a mix of emotions. There was apology there. But was there also something else? A question begging for her to trust him?

She thought so.

And she did trust him. In fact, she cared about him more than she'd ever realized.

But with this gun to her head, it was hard to think clearly.

Sienna felt her limbs trembling. Anita remained behind her in the truck with the gun still raised.

And Sienna had no idea how all of this would play out. What Devin would do.

Certainly he wouldn't grab Colby and bring him back. He would know better than to do that. Colby's life was more important than Sienna's.

And two hours was a long time to wait to see this to a conclusion.

It would be nearly dawn by then. Certainly someone else would head down this road and find them.

"Why are you doing this, Anita?" Sienna asked, trying to pass the time but to also get answers to the headache-inducing questions she'd been wrestling with. "It just doesn't make sense. You kidnapped Colby. I get that. You couldn't have kids, and you want them. But why did you leave him with me and go through this whole process of trying to get him back? It doesn't make sense."

"I'm sorry, Sienna. I really did think you were nice. And that made you the perfect target, unfortunately."

"Why'd you leave him with me?" Sienna repeated.

"I had to have surgery," Anita said. "I was injured when I was in the military, and my body hasn't been the same since then. My doctor told me if I didn't have this surgery, I would eventually die. I put it off for as long as I could."

"So you left Colby with me to have surgery yourself. Your mom wasn't involved."

"That's right. But while I was recovering in the hospital, Lisa Daniel tracked me down. She was on to me. I knew she would tell the police soon, too."

"I tried to call, but you didn't answer your phone. I don't understand."

"I wasn't able to come get Colby myself, and I was sure you wouldn't hand him over to my friend Justin. I sent Justin over to take him back."

"But that only caused the police to look for you even more. It doesn't make sense."

"That's the way it had to be!" Sweat sprinkled across her forehead. Sienna could see it in the rearview mirror. "I needed to disappear again and make a new life for myself. I didn't have time for niceties or to wrap up my life here. I had to move, and I had to move right then."

"But Justin wasn't able to snatch Colby that night."

Anita frowned menacingly. "No, you guys had to fight back and mess up everything. So we had to follow you guys, waiting for another opportunity."

"You left that tracking tile in the diaper bag so you could track us. You must have planned this from the beginning."

"That tile was always in the bag. It was the cheapest type of insurance I could think of. That way, if anything ever happened to Colby, I could find him—as long as the battery didn't die."

"Even when you knew Colby wasn't with us, you kept following us. You even made up a story about us and told people at that restaurant."

"We just needed to slow you down until we could figure out a plan. We realized we weren't getting into that headquarters of Jennings Center without you guys, though."

"And who is this Justin guy? Your boyfriend?"

"We've been together for ten years. He loves me and would do anything for me."

"You rescued him from the woods when we tied him up?"

"Of course I did. Did you think I'd leave him?"

"So you were there also."

"I got there late, but yes, I was there. I would have taken you both down, but I had to rescue my Justin."

"Where is Justin now?"

Anita smiled—a satisfied smile. "He's in the woods keeping an eye on your friend. I'd hate for him to break his promise."

A cold shiver rushed up Sienna's spine.

TWENTY-FOUR

Devin sloshed down the road. Rain pelted him, washing into his eyes and causing his clothing to cling to him. Every time he blinked, he pictured the gun Anita had to Sienna's head. His gut squeezed with apprehension. Would Anita really shoot Sienna?

He knew the answer.

She would.

The woman was unhinged and desperate. Nothing would stand in her way—not even someone she cared about like Justin.

Devin needed a plan, and he needed a plan quickly if he wanted to save both Sienna and Colby.

No way would he turn over Colby. But no way could Devin let Sienna get shot, either.

He took another step down the dark, desolate road and paused, glancing around. He looked for a sign of anything out of place, anything that his subconscious picked up on as a potential danger. He saw nothing.

Was someone in the forest? Watching him?

It was dark, and the rain was blinding. If someone was there, he'd be nearly impossible to spot.

The unease continued to churn in his gut, but he hadn't seen anyone. But the rain pelted the ground and the darkness made it impossible to see.

But the sound he'd heard had been a break from the normal noises around him. It had cut through the pounding rain, subtle but it had been there.

There it was again. A crack...almost like a stick had broken under an unseen weight.

What if Anita had Justin out here? What if Devin was being watched to ensure he did exactly as Anita said?

That would only make all of this even more complicated.

Devin didn't like complicated.

Nor did he like the fact that Anita had a gun to Sienna's head.

Sienna...his breath caught as he thought about her again. When all this was over, he was going to abandon the strongholds that held him back. Life was too short for that. Devin was going to tell Sienna that he wanted more for his future. That he found her fascinating. That he was beginning to feel the first pulses of love.

He shook his head. No, it was too early for that. Or was it?

Grace had always said when you knew, you knew.

And, if Devin were honest with himself, he knew.

But he had to deal with that later. Right now Devin had to ensure everyone survived. Otherwise, nothing else would matter.

As the rain came down harder, a realization hit him, something he should have thought about earlier.

If Devin couldn't see someone watching him, they couldn't see him, either.

Making a swift decision, he darted into the woods.

Devin was going to circle back around and sneak up on this man.

He reminded himself that he had no weapons. Devin was at a definite disadvantage, but he had to see what he could do here.

Because Colby and Sienna's lives depended on it. And he wouldn't lose someone else in his life to tragedy. Not if he could prevent it.

Cold fear caused a shiver to run down Sienna's spine as she stared straight ahead, waiting for whatever would happen next. She was keenly aware of the gun on the other side of the seat.

Aware that one flinch, one jerk of the finger, and she would be dead.

Her thoughts shifted to Devin. She wondered where he was. What he was doing. What he was thinking.

He was capable and strong. Certainly he'd come up with a plan, and she'd see him again when this was all done. They'd talk things through. Maybe even talk about a future together.

Sienna couldn't just sit here with her thoughts. No, she had to use this time wisely. Find out what she could. Maybe try to formulate some kind of plan.

Sienna glanced in the rearview mirror. She'd angled it so she could see Anita in the back seat and keep an eye on the situation. But she wondered if that was even wise when she saw the crazy, detached look in Anita's eyes.

"So now we just wait," Sienna said, crossing her arms and trying to sound braver than she felt.

"That's right. Now we wait."

"And once you have Colby?" Sienna knew without a doubt that Devin would not be bringing Colby here. Even the thought of it was sickening.

"Once I have Colby, I'll take what's rightfully mine—this truck—and Justin and I will leave." Spittle flew from Anita's mouth as she spoke.

"We'll start our new lives. Except this time, I won't let any nosy reporter stop me."

"How did Lisa Daniel discover you, anyway?" Sienna remembered some of the details, but she wanted to find out more from Anita. She wanted to keep her talking. Maybe it would help her keep her sanity.

"She just had to come into the school to do that article." Anita's face balled with anger and bitterness. "As soon as she saw me, I saw the flash of recognition in her gaze and knew it was only a matter of time before she put everything together."

"So the meeting at school was just random, a coincidence?" Sienna didn't believe in coincidences, but Anita didn't have to know that.

"Apparently the girl does freelance for a few newspapers and takes whatever stories she can get. Then she works on the pieces she's really passionate about on the side and sells them. I did all the research on her. She thought she was so smart." Her voice changed from bitter to satisfied. "But we showed her."

"By killing her and burning her body beyond recognition and adding your necklace to throw everyone off?" Sienna felt sick to her stomach even thinking about it.

"That's right." There wasn't even a hint of remorse in her voice.

"But I don't understand why you sent me those

messages once I went on the run, trying to protect Colby. Why did you tell me not to trust the police?" It truly confounded Sienna. As far as she knew, the police had nothing to do with this.

"I was hoping if you didn't get them involved, it would buy me more time. I also figured you might think I was running from an abusive ex or something. It was the most logical conclusion. I needed to give you something to think about and, in the meantime, buy myself more time."

"You really thought of everything, didn't you?" There was no admiration in her voice, not by a long shot. Only disgust. It took a truly twisted person to enact a plan like this.

"You have to get ahead and get what you want. This whole putting others above yourself? It's for the dogs. Look where it's left you." Anita let out a demeaning snicker.

"I was trying to help you, Anita." Sienna's teeth gritted together as her fear turned into anger. How could Anita be so heartless? Where was this woman's moral compass? Her compassion? The fact that she had neither of those things was terrifying.

"I know. And I'm saying you only need to help yourself."

"That's a sad way to live." As soon as Sienna said the words, she wondered if they'd been a good idea. But it was too late to take them back. She hadn't been trying to provoke Anita, but it wouldn't take much given her current mental state.

Anita suddenly grabbed Sienna's hair and jerked her head back. Pain shot through Sienna and a burning agony exploded on her scalp as she sucked in a gasp.

"You know what I think is sad?" Anita growled, still pulling Sienna's hair. "Not getting what you want in life. Having one accident mess everything up for you. How some people are handed everything on a silver platter while others are left destitute. That's not fair. You wouldn't understand."

"You're right." Sienna gritted her teeth as she spoke, trying to stave off the pain. "I can see where that doesn't seem fair. But don't think I'm one of those people who's been handed things. My dad worked at a factory, and I had to pay my own way through college. Everything I have, I've earned through hard work."

"Cry me a river. You're smart. You're pretty. Guys like you. Me, on the other hand? I'm broken. Overweight. And I have no money. So there you go."

"That doesn't mean that your life doesn't have potential." She wasn't going to accept Anita's explanation. Everyone had choices in life. Everyone.

"Oh, save me the pep talk. I'm long past that,

Sienna." She let go of Sienna, and Sienna's head jerked forward.

Sienna rubbed the back of her scalp, the seriousness of the situation weighing heavily on her. This could get a lot worse before it got better. *If* it got better. No, she couldn't think like that. It *would* get better.

As Sienna looked up, something appeared in the rearview mirror.

Lights.

Headlights.

A car was coming this way, Sienna realized.

Hope collided with fear inside her. Sienna prayed that no one would be hurt. That help might be in sight. And that Colby would be spared any more dealings with this twisted, heartless woman.

TWENTY-FIVE

Devin paused in the woods and waited for the rain to subside. As soon as the torrents died down, he waited. Listened.

A few minutes later, he heard more twigs cracking under someone's weight.

The man who was watching him.

Justin Henderson, most likely.

As soon as Devin figured out the direction the sounds came from, he cut back deeper in the woods. He watched his steps, careful not to give away his presence. No, the element of surprise was essential right now.

The sun would soon begin to peek through the morning sky. The realization made Devin move faster.

The ground was soggy, and the rocks he had to cross were slippery from the rain. The last thing he needed was to be clumsy or careless. He couldn't let a mistake slip him up.

Once he got twenty feet back, Devin paused and peered around the tree.

There he was.

Justin Henderson.

The man crouched near the road, gun in hand. He moved—almost slid along—parallel to the road. And, based on the way he glanced around, his head flickering back and forth, he was confused.

The man had realized he'd lost Devin.

Devin was going to have to make his move soon. The clock was counting down, and every moment Sienna was with Anita was a moment too long.

Moving swiftly but quietly, Devin approached Justin from behind.

The man had no idea he was coming.

As soon as Devin was close enough, he reached his arm around the man's neck and put the man in a chokehold.

Justin struggled against Devin's grip, trying to force Devin off him. But the man was also injured with a sling on his arm—probably from the gunshot wound Devin had given him. There was no way he'd be able to fight Devin off.

"Just stop fighting it," Devin said. "Make this easier."

The man didn't listen and continued to struggle, letting out little moans and grunts, like he was trying to respond but couldn't.

Three minutes later, the man slithered to the ground, passed out. Working quickly, Devin snatched his gun and his cell phone.

As he took the man's phone, a message appeared on the screen.

What's going on? Do you still see him?

That had to be from Anita.

Devin considered his response. He had to respond. Otherwise, the woman would get suspicious. Finally, he typed:

Everything is going according to plan. How about on your end?

He waited to see what she would say. A moment later, another message popped up. He wiped the rain from the screen to better read it.

I'm ready for this to be over. Don't let me down. You know I don't like it when people disappoint.

What did that mean? Devin didn't know, but it didn't sound good. He jammed the phone in his pocket.

He glanced back down at Justin. The man would be out for a while, and Devin had nothing to tie him up with. He was going to have to take that chance.

With that thought in mind, he took off at a fast clip back toward Sienna. As he moved, he used the man's phone to call Jenson and apprise him of what was happening.

"I don't like this," Jenson said.

Devin dodged around a boulder. "We need all the help we can get."

"I'm sending my men out there now. Try to hold them off until we can arrive."

"Will do."

Devin paused at the tree line, and the truck came into view. He spotted two people inside.

Anita and Sienna.

But, just then, another car had pulled up behind them.

A police car.

What? Had Jenson's guys gotten here already? That didn't seem possible.

How was Devin going to manage this?

Devin wasn't sure what was going on.

He glanced at his watch. Anita was expecting him back in forty-five minutes.

He had to figure things out soon.

"You ladies okay?" the officer asked, pointing a flashlight in the truck.

Red and blue lights flashed behind them, nearly blinding Sienna in the mirror. Anita had muttered threats as the officer approached, making it clear what would happen if Sienna messed up. One wrong move, and there would be consequences. Anita didn't need to spell out what those consequences would be. She could imagine them all too vividly.

Sienna waited for Anita to speak.

"We're fine, Officer." Anita's voice turned sugary sweet, along with her smile. "The road is blocked, and we're trying to figure out what to do. Our friend went to check out the options."

"Where are you headed?" The officer was a small-boned man with a pointy nose. Sienna would guess he was a rookie—maybe only in his early twenties. And he seemed clueless right now.

"The Jennings Center," Anita said. "My friend here just got a job there, and we're supposed to be there at 6:00 a.m. on the dot."

"You were going to be early…" The officer glanced at the tree. "Or maybe not."

"Exactly. My mom always said to plan ahead. It may not matter in this situation."

Anita sounded so normal right now that it was unnerving. She was a master manipulator, wasn't she?

"Well, the Jennings Center is a good place, so I wish you the best." He pointed his flashlight toward the tree. "But this is going to take a while to move. I'll call the city in, and they'll send a crew out. But it will be a couple of hours. If I were you, I'd call in and tell your new boss what's going on. I hate to make you late on the first day, but…"

"I understand, Officer," Sienna said. "I think I'll do just that."

"Okay, I just wanted to make sure everything is good. This storm has been a doozy. No one expected the high winds."

Sienna felt her blood pressure rising. The officer was chatty, yet Sienna was keenly aware that Anita had a gun pointed at her on the other side of the seat.

Yet Sienna stared at the officer, trying to send him a subliminal message that all wasn't well here. He obviously wasn't getting it.

"You two take care." The officer patted the side of the door and strolled back to his car.

Sienna released the breath she held. On one hand, she'd wanted the man to help. On the other hand, she'd envisioned worst-case scenarios. Anita could have shot him if the situation escalated. Then she could have shot Sienna.

She really had no idea how all of this was going to play out. But she had to keep the faith.

She had to stay strong and believe that somehow, some way, she could find her way out of this horrible situation. Even if she didn't, her prayer would be the same as Daniel's from the

Bible—even if God didn't save her, He was still good.

She only hoped Colby remained safe. That was the important thing.

"You got lucky on that one," Anita said, her sweet voice disappearing as easily as flipping a switch. "I thought I was going to have to add one more person to my body count."

Sienna shifted uncomfortably in the front seat, glad it hadn't come to that. She wasn't sure if Anita was referring to the officer or Sienna. It didn't matter. One more death—whoever it might be—would be too many.

"What are you going to do once you get Colby, Anita?"

She didn't think Anita would actually get her hands on the boy, but she wanted to get inside the woman's head and figure out what she was thinking. It was only smart.

"I'll take him somewhere new and start again. Start fresh. Maybe we'll really have a chance this time."

"Like where?" Sienna knew if Anita shared information on an exact location, that meant Anita planned on killing Sienna. There was no way she'd tell her otherwise.

She held her breath as she waited to see how Anita would respond.

"Somewhere far away," Anita said, her eyes taking on a distant look.

"I see." So maybe Anita didn't plan on killing her. A brief flash of relief rushed through her.

"I was thinking about Alaska. I've always wanted to see that part of the country."

Sienna's stomach clenched. That flash of relief was premature. Anita didn't plan on letting Sienna walk away from this.

"Did you befriend me from the beginning with the intent of using me like this?" Sienna asked, trying to ignore the tremble in her voice.

"I hoped it wouldn't come to this. I mean, I really did like you. Everyone likes you. How could they not? You're Ms. Perfect." Anita's face clouded like she had a bad taste in her mouth.

"I'm far from perfect."

Anita didn't seem to hear her. "But then that reporter showed up, and I knew everything was over. I could see the recognition in her eyes. I had to come up with a plan. I could see how kind you were, and I knew you were the best chance of finding someone to help me."

"I see. So kindness is a weakness." Sienna just couldn't understand the way this woman thought.

"Your kindness made you a target. I'm really sorry I had to do this to you, Sienna. I am. But nothing is going to separate me from my child. Nothing."

Sienna swallowed hard and tried to choose her words wisely. She kept her voice even as she said, "He's not your child, Anita."

Anita's eyes flashed with anger. "He *is* my child! And he always will be! Just because I didn't give birth to him doesn't mean he's not mine."

Sienna licked her lips. "What about the Brightons?"

"I feel badly for them, but we all can't have Colby. This is just the way it has to be."

"Why'd you pick him?"

Anita shrugged. "Because he was adorable."

"And how did you manage to snatch him without leaving any evidence behind?"

"They left their keys in the diaper bag one day. I sneaked away during my lunch break and made a copy. Easy-peasy. Now, I'm tired of talking. Your boyfriend has forty minutes to get back here. I really hope I don't have to enact the second part of my plan."

"The second part of your plan?" Sienna's throat tightened. She wasn't sure she wanted to know.

"That's right, sweetie." Anita smiled, but the action lacked any sincerity. "That's the part where you die."

As Devin watched the police officer pull away, he had a change of plans.

He couldn't simply confront Anita. No, that would never work.

He needed leverage.

With that thought in mind, he hurried through the woods back to Justin and shook him. The man's eyes fluttered open as he startled awake.

"What? Where? How—"

Devin jerked the man to his feet and showed him the gun. "There's no time for questions. Just walk."

"Where are you taking me?" Justin tried to shake him off and pull away.

Devin wasn't going to let that happen. "You'll see."

He shoved the gun harder into Justin's side to remind him it was there.

He led the man back to the downed tree in the road. Remaining in the woods, they walked behind the trees and well out of sight.

"You can't do this," Justin said. "Angela is smart. She's not going to let you get away with this."

"Is that right?"

"Yeah, man. You have no idea what you're doing. We're all going to end up dead."

The man looked like he was over it. This wasn't his mission, Devin realized. No, Justin was just acting as Anita's minion, and he looked on the verge of giving up.

"You love her?" Devin asked.

"Angela? Yeah, of course I do. I don't know what I'd do without her."

"You're willing to go to jail for her."

He kept his chin up. "I'd do anything for her."

"Sounds like true love then," Devin muttered. "Now we're going to see how much she loves you. I have a feeling she doesn't share the sentiment as much as you think."

Justin stared back, his lips parting with surprise. "Of course she does."

"Then why didn't she leave Colby with you when she had her surgery?"

"Because…because…it just made more sense. I've never raised a kid before."

"Keep thinking that."

Moving swiftly, he shoved Justin until they were at the truck window. Then he hit the glass with his gun.

"Get out of the car, Anita," Devin ordered.

Anita jerked her head toward them, her eyes widening as the processed what was happening. Her expression morphed from surprised to angry.

"Justin…" She cracked the window. "You're back. Where's Colby? What's going on?"

"I'm calling the shots now. Let Sienna go, and I'll spare your boyfriend." Devin glanced over. Saw Sienna. Saw that she was okay.

Relief filled him.

That was enough. For now. Devin just needed to know she was still alive and not hurt. He'd deal with the rest of the details later.

"You're out of your mind. Don't you remember what I told you?" Anita's nostrils flared.

"Oh, I remember. But you're not getting Colby."

"I'll be the one who decides that," Anita said.

"Get out of the truck, Anita, or I'll shoot Justin." Devin was tired of letting Anita think that she had the upper hand here.

With a scowl, Anita climbed out, pulling Sienna behind her. Sienna's face twisted with pain as her weight came down on her leg.

Anita didn't care. She kept the gun at Sienna's side, near her heart. One pull of the trigger, and everything would be over for Sienna.

Devin's heart pounded with agony at the thought. He couldn't let that happen. He had to keep control of this situation.

"Now, let's do a trade," Devin said. "You give me Sienna, and you can have Justin. You two can go on your merry way, and we'll pretend this didn't happen."

Devin knew he couldn't let this go like that. But he had to get Sienna back somehow.

Colby was safe. Colby would remain safe as long as he stayed with Rick and Trina.

"That's not going to happen." Anita's voice came out as a low grumble. "I want my baby."

"You can't have Colby."

"I will get Colby. He's mine."

"You need to think this through, Anita."

"Anita, just let Sienna go," Justin said. "We'll think of another way."

"There is no other way!" The woman sounded

on the verge of losing it—even more than she had earlier.

"There's always another way," Justin continued, his voice pleading. "We've been through so much. Let's just go away and start again."

"Not without Colby."

"He's going to kill me, Anita. If he doesn't kill me, he'll send me away to jail for the rest of my life."

"They won't catch us. Now stop talking!"

"They will catch us. I'm tired of running. I've done everything you've said. Now it's time to move on."

"Listen to yourself! Can you hear how pathetic you sound? I thought I was dating a man. Now I realize that you're just a boy."

"No, I'm a man who's trying to use his head right now. We're in over our heads. Enough is enough. Please. Please."

Anita's scowl deepened. "Now you're relying on cowardice. Do you know how much I hate cowards?"

"It's not cowardly to want the woman you love to be safe," Justin said. "Let's just talk this through."

"There's nothing to talk through," Anita growled.

In an instant, she raised her gun and fired.

TWENTY-SIX

Sienna gasped as she watched Justin fall to the ground.

Anita had just shot him.

She'd *shot* him.

Sienna could hardly breathe as she peered down at the man, her heart racing out of control. Using her other hand, she wiped her rain-drenched eyes.

Justin lay on the ground, gasping and clutching his chest. His expression showed his agony as he croaked out one word. "Why?"

Anita sneered, leaning closer. "Because you have no backbone. I can't trust you anymore. You're not in this with me."

"I…loved…you," he said, his breathing heavier and more labored with each passing second.

Then his eyes went still, his body stiff, and Sienna knew he was dead.

If this woman would kill her boyfriend in cold blood, she wouldn't think twice about killing

Sienna or Devin. Sienna didn't find comfort in the thought.

Anita's gun was back at her side, and she turned to Devin. "Did you really think that was going to work?"

Devin's jaw visibly tightened. "You're more coldhearted than I gave you credit for."

"I told you, nothing is going to stand in my way. Especially not a man. Now we're going to have to do something else here, aren't we?" She jammed the gun into Sienna's temple until Sienna yelped.

Trembles raced through her. Just what was running through Anita's head? Sienna wouldn't put anything past her.

And that thought was terrifying.

"There's no need to do anything else drastic here," Devin said, lowering his gun.

"Give me your gun," Anita demanded.

"Killing us won't get you anywhere." Devin squatted to the ground and placed his gun there. A calming tone overtook his voice.

"No, I need to use you first and then kill you," she said with a satisfied smile. "Don't worry. I've thought this through. I've had nothing better to do as I've been recovering from surgery. But I didn't give you enough credit, Sienna. I thought you'd be easier to manipulate. But time after time you've thwarted whatever my plans were. Not this time."

"It doesn't have to be this way, Anita," Sienna said, still keenly aware of the gun at her head. "You need help. Colby needs his parents."

"I'm his parent!" Anita smacked the gun across Sienna's face. "And I never want to hear you say otherwise again!"

Sienna grasped her cheek, feeling a new ache forming. Pain radiated from the point of impact, and she tasted blood in her mouth.

Devin's gaze caught hers, and Sienna saw the concern there. Saw that he wanted to reach for her. To help.

But they were at the mercy of this woman— this crazy woman.

"Now we're going to have to do things the hard way," Anita growled. "We need to start walking. And if you try anything again, FBI man, I will kill her."

Anita stared at Devin until he nodded.

As Sienna took a step forward, pain radiated up her leg. Her face ached. She wasn't sure she could make this walk in her current state. She had no choice but to try.

How were they going to get out of this now?

Sienna had no idea.

But she really hoped that Devin had some kind of plan.

Devin's heart ached when he saw the pain Sienna was in. It wasn't just physical pain. It was emotional and mental. This situation would test every part of them.

A person didn't quickly recover from seeing someone die in front of them—even if the person was an enemy. Plus, Anita was so desperate to get Colby back that she'd become hyperfocused. The woman wasn't even frantic, which made her even scarier. No, she didn't seem to feel much at all. She just wanted Colby.

Devin hadn't anticipated Anita shooting Justin. He'd thought the woman had cared about him, that she'd loved the man. But all she obviously cared about was herself.

And that made this even more difficult.

"We're going to have to go around the tree," Anita said. "Try anything funny, and you're both dead. But first you'll watch Sienna die. It's always a horrible thing to witness, isn't it, FBI Agent Matthews? Having a loved one pass away and feeling helpless to do anything about it…"

His spine clenched. So Anita had done her research. She knew about Grace and Willow. And the fact she was gloating about it only made his blood boil even more.

"Move!" Anita demanded, shoving Sienna to the side of the road.

Sienna let out a gasp and started to reach for her leg when Anita jerked her upright.

"This is no time to be a wuss!" Anita yelled.

"She's hurt." Devin's heart leaped into his throat. "Let me help her."

"She'll manage fine on her own."

"I don't think she will. She's hurt." Devin had seen Sienna limping along and knew she was in agony. He wanted nothing more than to help her.

He should have insisted that she be checked out earlier, right after she'd cut her leg and they'd gotten out of the woods. Maybe they wouldn't be in this mess if he had. But it was too late to go back.

"You can hold on to her arm," Anita finally said. "Or she can hold on to your arm. But that's it. I just can't afford for her to slow us up."

Devin extended his hand to Sienna, and she took it, holding on to it like a crutch as she limped forward. It felt good to touch her. To have her close. He only wished he could offer more.

He looked into the distance. The rain was starting to let up some, and the first signs of dawn were beginning to show on the horizon.

Hopefully backup would be here soon. But, even when help did arrive, it would be hard to reach them with that tree in the road.

"What's your plan?" Devin asked, trying to get inside Anita's mind.

If he knew what she was planning, maybe he could stop her.

Maybe.

"You're going to get me inside the complex,"

Anita said. "And then if I have to shoot everyone in sight to get to my boy, I will. I have two hostages that will be killed if people don't get out of my way."

The bad feeling in Devin's gut only grew in intensity.

He had no doubt the woman was telling the truth. She wasn't going to stop at anything until she had Colby back.

Dear Lord, I could use some wisdom right about now.

He heard Sienna moan beside him and glanced over. Her face was stretched tight with pain.

He'd been crazy not to swoop this woman away when he'd had the chance. And, as soon as he did have the chance, he was going to tell Sienna that. If the thought of losing Sienna shook him up this much, then Devin knew it was time to act on his feelings.

Grace would approve. Deep in his gut, he knew she would. It had taken all this for him to know for sure.

"I'm sorry," he whispered to Sienna.

She quickly glanced up at him, her face cinched with pain. "For what?"

"For holding back. When this is over…"

She squeezed his hand. "Tell me when it's over. You're going to have the chance. We can't think differently."

He pulled his gaze away from her and nodded. "You're right. We will."

He wouldn't tell her goodbye. Not now. This wasn't over yet.

"Stop chatting, you two," Anita muttered. "We're almost there."

Devin looked in the distance. Sure enough, the entrance to the Jennings Center waited ahead.

He cringed at the thought of anyone else getting hurt. He couldn't let that happen. Yet he couldn't get close enough to Anita to take her down. She was on edge, and her gun was aimed at Sienna. It was too risky to approach her until he had a clear opportunity—and he didn't.

Just as they were ten feet in front of the entrance, something ran from the woods.

Before Devin could see what it was, Anita screamed.

It was a bear, Devin realized.

A black bear.

And it was headed toward Anita.

TWENTY-SEVEN

Sienna watched in horror as the bear charged toward Anita. The woman seemed to forget what was happening and took off in a run. The bear ran after her.

"Devin…" Sienna whispered, fear sweeping through her.

"Come on." He grabbed Anita's gun—she'd dropped it—and then swooped Sienna up in his arms. He ran with her toward the gate, where a guard stood, looking puzzled at the turn of events.

"I'm Special Agent Devin Matthews. Rick and Trina are my good friends, and we need your help."

"Come on in." He nodded them through.

Devin placed Sienna on the ground before stepping out of the gate and closing it.

Panic raced through her. "Devin, no! What are you doing?"

"I have to make sure Anita doesn't get away again," he said. "I have to end this."

"But the bear…"

"I'll handle the bear. And the police are on the way. It's going to be okay." He went back to gate and pressed his face into it. "Sienna, I love you."

She let out a little cry, her face in front of his. She desperately wished she could hold him now. But she couldn't. "I love you, too, Devin."

He leaned between the bars and planted a soft kiss on her lips.

Sienna felt herself melting. Something had changed in Devin. She'd sensed him wrestling with his inner thoughts. The wrestling match must finally be over, and he'd decided what would win.

Sienna looked over his shoulder as Anita screamed. The bear still chased Anita, and the woman ran across the road with her arms in the air.

For a moment, her heart panged with compassion for the woman. Even after everything she'd done…it was hard to see someone so terrified.

It looked like that man at the cabin had been right when he'd said there were a lot of bears in the area lately. And it was dawn, so they were coming out now to feed.

Devin turned toward the scene.

He raised his gun in the air and fired.

The bear froze. Rose up on his two hind legs.

Sienna held her breath, waiting to see what would happen next.

The bear remained still upright a moment and then…he darted back into the woods.

As soon as the creature had disappeared, Devin jogged across the pavement to Anita, who'd collapsed onto the ground. Her shoulders heaved with exertion and fear.

"Looks like your plan didn't work out so well after all," he muttered, grabbing her arm.

"Shut up," Anita grumbled. "Nobody could have planned for that."

Devin jerked the woman to her feet and dragged her toward the gate. "You're coming with me."

No sooner had he done that than police filled the area. They must have filtered in behind the downed tree.

Jenson stepped forward, leading the charge. He had cuffs in his hand, and he headed right toward Anita.

"I'll take it from here," he said. "Good work."

With that, Devin hurried back to Sienna.

Maybe this nightmare was finally over. Maybe.

Two hours later, the majority of law enforcement had cleared away. Devin and Sienna stood on a lovely patio area in the center of the Jennings Center compound. Despite everything, the day had turned out beautiful.

Paramedics had come and checked out both of them. They would be okay, and their bodies would heal in time from any of the injuries they'd received today. Trina had brought them coffee and muffins, and they'd been able to take a shower and change.

Sienna felt one hundred times better.

She still hadn't seen Colby, but the boy was sleeping. She wanted to let him rest. But just seeing his sleeping figure had filled her with such peace.

He was okay. He was really okay.

This was the first moment she and Devin had alone. As soon as Devin stepped toward her, she instinctively fell into his arms.

"I'm so glad you're okay," she murmured to his chest. She didn't want to ever let go. Ever.

He kissed the top of her head. "I'm glad you're okay, too, and that we can finally put this behind us."

She looked up at him, her eyes glistening. There were things she needed to say. Important things. "I don't know what I would have done without you."

"Sienna, about what I said earlier, after I kissed you—"

"I know you just miss your wife and daughter," she said quickly, remembering his agonizing apology. "I understand."

He lowered his head and voice as he stepped

closer to her. "The thing is, I know I need to move on. That it's time. I've just been…afraid, I suppose."

She heard the unmistakable sound of affection in his voice and rested her hand against his chest. "I didn't think men like you were ever afraid."

"Believe me, we're afraid plenty. We just have to push past it."

"And that's what makes you brave." She smiled at him, reaching up and skimming her fingers across his jaw. "I like that."

"I was hoping you would." His gaze went to her lips, her eyes and back to her lips.

He leaned forward until their lips touched. This time, there was no apology. No, it was only bliss. Pure bliss.

"You guys," someone said. "Oh, sorry."

They pulled away from each other and looked over. Trina stood there, an apologetic look on her face.

"I didn't mean to interrupt," she said, grinning feverishly.

"Is everything okay?" Devin asked, his hands still at Sienna's waist.

"It's Colby. He's awake. I thought you'd want to see him."

Devin took Sienna's hand and led her inside and down the hallway. Sienna stepped into Colby's temporary bedroom and peered into his crib.

He lay there with a smile on his face.

He was okay, she realized.

After all of this, he really was okay. Happy. Healthy. No worse for the wear.

As he reached out his arms, Sienna swept him into her embrace. His baby-clean scent surrounded her, and gratitude filled her.

There were times she'd doubted the ending of all this. She was so glad to be standing here now.

She carried him into the living room so he could wake up. He had a big day ahead of him.

Fifteen minutes later, a car pulled up outside. Devin and Sienna stepped out to greet the people inside. Before they even made it down the steps, two people came running from the back seat.

The Brightons.

Detective Jenson had sent for them.

"Where's Liam?" Joyce asked, nearly breathless. "Please, can we see him?"

Anita had admitted she took the baby from the couple. There could be some other formalities the Brightons would have to go through, but these people deserved to see their baby. The family deserved to be reunited.

"Follow me," Devin said.

He led them inside Rick and Trina's house. As he opened the door, Trina stood there with a smiling Colby in her arms.

Joyce and George nearly melted with happiness and tears.

Colby seemed to instinctively know the couple. He reached his arms out to them. Joyce wrapped the boy in her embrace and hugged him as she sobbed with joy.

Sienna smiled as she watched the scene. There were happy endings. She hoped she would have one herself. With Devin.

As if on cue, he appeared beside her, wrapping his arm around her waist.

Life had been a nightmare over the past few days, but something beautiful had come from all the pain.

And today, a family had been reunited—Sienna glanced at Devin—and maybe a new one was on the verge of forming.

TWENTY-EIGHT

Six months later

Sienna turned away from the freestanding mirror after double-checking that her gown was in place. It was not only in place—it was fabulous.

The simple white bodice fit her perfectly. She wore a small clip in the back of her hair with rows of tulle tucked underneath, pearls stretched around her neck and beneath the billows of her skirt, she'd donned white Converse sneakers. When she put it all together, the look summed her up nicely.

Sienna had never wanted a fancy wedding. No, this ceremony with only her closest family and friends at a small, traditional church in the mountains was exactly what she'd always envisioned.

Just like Devin was who she'd always envisioned being by her side—for life.

Someone knocked at the door to her make-shift dressing room, and she called, "Come in!"

Devin stepped inside, looking dapper in his black tuxedo. He let out a low whistle as he closed the door behind him. "You look gorgeous."

She curtsied. "Thank you. You look handsome yourself—even if you're not supposed to be in here. Don't you know the rules?"

As Devin stepped closer, Sienna straightened his collar, her heart feeling so full that it could burst. She couldn't wait to spend the rest of her life with this man.

"I thought maybe we could pray together before the ceremony," he said. "I thought it would be the perfect way to start this day—to start the rest of our lives together." He brushed his knuckles softly across her cheek.

Sienna's heart warmed even more. "I think that's a great idea. And here I was afraid that you were getting cold feet."

"Never." He smiled reassuringly.

Sienna still couldn't believe it. Couldn't believe that she was getting married. Couldn't believe that Devin had turned out to be the man of her dreams.

Gone was the brooding neighbor who isolated himself. Everyone said he was back to being the person he used to be—back before tragedy had altered his world—and she really liked this Devin.

The two of them had decided to buy a house away from their original neighborhood, somewhere they could make new memories together. They'd sold their furniture and purchased new items, ready for a fresh start.

Sienna couldn't wait to dive into her new life.

Anita was going on trial next month, but everyone knew the case would be a slam dunk. The body in the woods had turned out to be Lisa's. Her name was mentioned in the subsequent news articles, giving her credit for helping to solve the case. And Colby—Liam—was doing great.

"Hey, you two! You're not supposed to see each other before the ceremony," Viviana said, stepping into the room in a lovely wine-colored bridesmaid's dress.

"We couldn't resist," Sienna said, keeping her hands at Devin's waist as she turned toward her friend.

"Oh, you guys are too cute. I couldn't be happier for you."

"Thanks, Viviana." Sienna smiled at her friend.

"I just came back here to let you know that your special guests have arrived."

Sienna drew in a deep breath of excitement. She'd asked Viviana to let her know. "Great. Can you send them back?"

Viviana's eyebrows shot up. "You don't want to wait until after the ceremony?"

"Absolutely not. I need to see them now."

"I'll send them back then. Your wish is my command."

A few minutes later, the Brightons appeared inside the old Sunday school classroom with the sky-blue walls. Sienna felt the smile spread across her face when she spotted Colby—or Liam, she should say. He'd always be Colby in her mind.

He'd gotten bigger since she'd last seen him a couple of months ago. And his hair was longer, and his smile wider. Overall, he looked like he was doing great.

"Hey there, sweet boy." Sienna leaned down to look at the boy's handsome face. "How are you?"

"Good…" He jabbed his finger into Joyce. "Mama."

Sienna smiled. "That's right. That's your mama."

Liam's finger then went into George's chest. "Dada."

"What a smart boy you are." Sienna took his hand into hers and kissed his little fingers. "A very smart, blessed boy."

"Yes, he is," George said.

Sienna swung her gaze back up to the couple. "I'm so glad you could come."

"We wouldn't have missed it," Joyce said. Her

face said it all—the gratitude she felt, along with thankfulness and completeness.

It was a beautiful sight.

"How are things going?" Devin asked.

"It's great," George said. "Honestly, it couldn't be better. Liam is happy, and he's adjusted well. We're staying in touch with a psychologist, just to make sure we're on track. But we couldn't be happier."

"That makes me happy." Sienna stepped back toward Devin, and his arm went around her waist again.

"We just want to say thank you again for everything you did," George said. "You both put your lives at risk to help us. I don't know how we could ever repay you."

"I'd hope someone would do it for us, if the roles were ever reversed."

"Sienna, it's time for the ceremony," Viviana said, peeking her head back inside. "I hate to break this up, but we have a crowd waiting for you."

"Thanks, Viviana."

"We'll let you two go," Joyce said. "We can't wait to see the ceremony, and we'll talk to you afterward."

"Sounds good. Bye, Liam."

The boy waved to Sienna, melting her heart yet again. He just had that effect on her.

When they were gone, Sienna turned toward Devin. "You ready for this?"

He leaned down and kissed her. "I've been ready. Now, about that prayer…"

"Of course."

They bowed their heads together as Devin began speaking. "Father in Heaven, we trust You for all of our days. Please bless this union. Make us stronger. Help me to be the man Sienna needs. Guard our hearts. Protect our relationship. And Lord, we praise You for bringing us together, even if it was in ways that we might have never foreseen."

As he said amen, Sienna was still smiling. Yes, God had definitely brought them together in a way Sienna would have never imagined.

But she was thankful for the good that had come from the bad.

"Okay, get out there, and I'll meet you on the stage," Sienna said. "And then…forever. You and me."

Devin grinned. "Forever. You and me. I like the sound of that."

* * * * *

Dear Reader,

Thank you so much for reading *The Cradle Conspiracy*. I hope you enjoyed Sienna and Devin's story and their journey to protect an innocent child. The challenge ahead of them felt overwhelming at times, but together they were able to overcome each obstacle.

Have you ever been placed in a situation where you felt like a mountain stood before you? Have you wondered how you would ever climb such an insurmountable problem and get to the other side?

I think we all feel like that at times. Aren't you thankful that our help comes from above and that we don't have to lean on our own understanding in the hard times? I know I'm grateful to serve a God who can move mountains in our lives.

When the journey feels tough and like the obstacles will never cease, remember there's Someone to help you every step of the way.

Blessings,
Christy Barritt

Get 4 FREE REWARDS!

We'll send you 2 FREE Books plus 2 FREE Mystery Gifts.

Love Inspired® books feature contemporary inspirational romances with Christian characters facing the challenges of life and love.

FREE Value Over $20

YES! Please send me 2 FREE Love Inspired® Romance novels and my 2 FREE mystery gifts (gifts are worth about $10 retail). After receiving them, if I don't wish to receive any more books, I can return the shipping statement marked "cancel." If I don't cancel, I will receive 6 brand-new novels every month and be billed just $5.24 for the regular-print edition or $5.99 each for the larger-print edition in the U.S., or $5.74 for the regular-print edition or $6.24 each for the larger-print edition in Canada. That's a savings of at least 13% off the cover price. It's quite a bargain! Shipping and handling is just 50¢ per book in the U.S. and $1.25 per book in Canada.* I understand that accepting the 2 free books and gifts places me under no obligation to buy anything. I can always return a shipment and cancel at any time. The free books and gifts are mine to keep no matter what I decide.

Choose one: ☐ **Love Inspired® Romance Regular-Print** (105/305 IDN GNWC) ☐ **Love Inspired® Romance Larger-Print** (122/322 IDN GNWC)

Name (please print)

Address   Apt. #

City   State/Province   Zip/Postal Code

Mail to the **Reader Service:**
IN U.S.A.: P.O. Box 1341, Buffalo, NY 14240-8531
IN CANADA: P.O. Box 603, Fort Erie, Ontario L2A 5X3

Want to try 2 free books from another series? Call 1-800-873-8635 or visit www.ReaderService.com.

*Terms and prices subject to change without notice. Prices do not include sales taxes, which will be charged (if applicable) based on your state or country of residence. Canadian residents will be charged applicable taxes. Offer not valid in Quebec. This offer is limited to one order per household. Books received may not be as shown. Not valid for current subscribers to Love Inspired Romance books. All orders subject to approval. Credit or debit balances in a customer's account(s) may be offset by any other outstanding balance owed by or to the customer. Please allow 4 to 6 weeks for delivery. Offer available while quantities last.

Your Privacy—The Reader Service is committed to protecting your privacy. Our Privacy Policy is available online at www.ReaderService.com or upon request from the Reader Service. We make a portion of our mailing list available to reputable third parties that offer products we believe may interest you. If you prefer that we not exchange your name with third parties, or if you wish to clarify or modify your communication preferences, please visit us at www.ReaderService.com/consumerschoice or write to us at Reader Service Preference Service, P.O. Box 9062, Buffalo, NY 14240-9062. Include your complete name and address.

LI19R3